Who Will Hear Your Secrets?

Johns Hopkins: Poetry and Fiction
John T. Irwin, General Editor

Who Will Hear Your Secrets?

Stories by Robley Wilson

THE JOHNS HOPKINS UNIVERSITY PRESS

Baltimore

This book has been brought to publication with the generous assistance of the G. Harry Pouder Fund and the Writing Seminars Publication Fund.

Published 2012
Printed in the United States of America on acid-free paper
2 4 6 8 9 7 5 3 1

The Johns Hopkins University Press
2715 North Charles Street
Baltimore, Maryland 21218-4363
www.press.jhu.edu

Library of Congress Cataloging-in-Publication Data

Wilson, Robley.
Who will hear your secrets? : stories / by Robley Wilson.
    p.   cm. — (Johns Hopkins, poetry and fiction)
ISBN-13: 978-1-4214-0462-2 (pbk. : acid-free paper)
ISBN-10: 1-4214-0462-1 (pbk. : acid-free paper)
    I. Title.
PS3573.I4665W47 2011
813'.54—dc23   2011026155

A catalog record for this book is available from
the British Library.

Special discounts are available for bulk purchases of this book. For more information, please contact Special Sales at 410-516-6936 or specialsales@press.jhu.edu.

The Johns Hopkins University Press uses environmentally friendly book materials, including recycled text paper that is composed of at least 30 percent post-consumer waste, whenever possible.

For Stephen Minot
(1927–2010)
friend & mentor

Contents

Who Will Hear Your Secrets?

The Dark

The first time Brian Varney, tourist, drove past the orange gate in the rented Opel, a number of automobiles were parked at the edges of the drive leading to the gate, and others were pulled off on both sides of the dirt road beyond. Brian counted seven cars in all.

"Whoever lives there is throwing a party," he told the woman beside him.

"So it seems," Delia said.

It was a Saturday evening, half past eight, the Irish sky still vividly alight as it would be until after ten, so the party hypothesis made sense. It was only in the following days that the two Americans realized the cars belonged to hikers, who parked them near a trail entrance in the morning and reclaimed them at the tired end of each day—long days, fifteen or sixteen hours in July.

They began to speculate about who lived behind the orange gate. Wealth was involved, Brian said, for you could see the several dormers of a rambling house that must hold a dozen rooms at least. Perhaps an Irish dot-com millionaire who cashed in before the market collapsed. Wealth, yes, Delia agreed, but inherited, a retired British couple choosing to settle in this evergreen countryside, safe from all social distractions save the occasional black-faced sheep trespassing innocently.

One noon they walked up the graveled drive for a closer inspection of the brightly painted gate. The gabled house seemed deserted; the only sound was of the wind in a grove of tall pines beyond. Beside the gate was a wooden kiosk, a kind of sentry box with an intercom system, the kiosk as orange as the gate itself. At either side of the gate, invisible from the road, barbed wire extended to left and right through the brush and goldenrod. Above that wire was another, thinner, attached to white porcelain insulators on fence posts in both directions.

"Let's not disturb these folks today," Brian said.

Delia punched him playfully on the arm. "Idiot," she said. "Were you seriously thinking of calling on them?"

"I thought it was a possibility," he said. "'Hello, we're renting the cottage just down the road. We thought we'd make a neighborly visit.'"

"Idiot," she said, and she punched his arm again.

"Don't," he said.

She took his hand as they strolled away from the gate. Halfway back to the road Brian pointed out a thin black cable laid across the drive.

"Early warning," he said. "This owner is super security-conscious. Maybe he's a retired godfather."

*　*　*

IN THE DAYS THAT FOLLOWED they did the usual: overnight trips to Galway, to Tipperary, to Killarney and the Ring of Kerry; a dreadful visit to Cork and its mad insular traffic; a tour of Waterford Crystal and a detour to Kinsale, where Brian had roots. Each night, in their rooms at one or another hotel or "modernized" castle, they went to bed early and read the *Irish Times*, trying to make heads and tails of events in the North—murders, petrol bombings, Protestant marches past Catholic ghettos; Unionists, R.U.C., Sinn Fein, I.R.A., splinters and spokesmen whose motives were baffling to them.

"I give up," Brian would say. "Screw both sides."

Then they switched off the lights and dreamed the dreams of tourists, which frequently involved the appearance of persons who had long been dead, and who spoke to them as if there were no boundary between death and life.

"Ancestors," he said one morning after they had shared their dreams.

"But no river of forgetfulness and no ferryman." That was Delia: literary to a fault.

So their holiday passed evenly and swiftly. When they woke in the morning, sometimes there was sun to make the dew glisten on the leaves of the buttercups behind the cottage. If there was rain instead—as often there was—the yellow blossoms bowed dully, the grasses around them laid flat with wet. On the dry mornings they went walking along the one-lane road that took them to a lay-by overlooking the lakes of Killarney, or through the fields in the shadow of Torc Mountain dotted with foxglove and daisy, dandelion and clover, the black-faced sheep on the trail jostling one another aside to avoid the walkers. They talked to the sheep, Brian especially. On the rainy days they drank coffee and played chess and made lazy love while Radio One did interviews and quizzes whose big prizes were always trips to Orlando or New York City.

Afternoons they drove to castles and waterfalls and mountain vistas. They photographed each other against the postcard backgrounds, drove to Tesco or Dunnes for their kitchen necessities. Late in the day they ate pub suppers and drank stout; if there was music, sometimes they stayed on into the evenings and drove home pleasantly but not dangerously drunk. They fell into bed secure in the knowledge that they had done—and would go on doing—exactly what American visitors were expected to do.

*   *   *

ONE MIDNIGHT, as they were driving home from the local pub, a deer emerged from the profusion of ferns alongside the road to the cottage. It stood at the roadside, ears alert, great eyes inquisitive, unmoving as stone. It was a fawn; in the oblique headlight of the stopped car its markings were like a double row of pale silver coins on the side turned toward them.

"Look how lovely," Delia said.

"I hope it doesn't decide to jump in front of us when we move on," Brian said.

He put the car in gear. The fawn remained motionless, watching as they went past.

"That was something," Delia said. "That was a high point."

Brian shifted into second, then third. He had never tried fourth gear on this road, partly because he would rather not be moving too fast if he met an oncoming car and had to veer left onto the overgrown slope. Still, the speedometer read 30 miles an hour, too fast for him to swerve or stop when another deer—this one not a fawn, but adult, perhaps half again the size of a big dog—appeared from beside the road and crossed close in front of him. The right front fender struck the animal; Brian saw it knocked down, exactly at the driveway to the orange gate, saw it in the headlight glare struggle to its feet in an awkwardness of delicate slender legs. He saw it run on up the drive and disappear.

"Jesus," Brian said.

"Oh, my God." Delia was clutching his shoulder with both hands.

"I couldn't stop. It just came out of nowhere."

"What do we do?"

"I don't know." He opened the glove compartment and took out

4

the flashlight they had brought from the cottage. "We don't know how badly it's hurt."

"But it jumped over that fence," Delia said.

"Did it really? Or did it just seem to? Maybe it plowed into the bushes in front of the fence."

"It looked like it went over."

Brian got out of the car.

"Oh, Brian." Delia got out of the car on her side and walked around to the front. The car idled; the headlights were still on. Brian was crouched at the fender that had struck the deer.

"The headlight glass is smashed," he said. "I don't see any blood."

"Maybe it's really all right."

Brian straightened up and switched off the flashlight. "Hop back in the car," he said.

"What are you going to do?"

"Tell whoever owns the house what happened."

"It's so late," she said. "We shouldn't disturb them."

"I'd hate to think of it just stumbling around in the woods. Maybe dying by degrees."

"It's fine," Delia said. "Really. It went over the fence."

"We have to tell somebody."

"What good will that do?"

But Brian shut his door, waited for Delia to shut hers, and turned the car into the driveway. "I can imagine what the rental-car people are going to stick us for that headlight," he said.

*　*　*

He stopped the car at the gate and got out. On the other side of the fence, light showed in the front windows of the house.

"They're awake in there." He said it over his shoulder to Delia, who stayed by the idling car.

At the front of the kiosk, sheltered from the elements under a miniature pitched roof, was a metal speaker, and beside the speaker was what looked like a doorbell. Brian pushed it. For a full minute nothing happened, so he pushed it again.

The speaker hummed and crackled. "Who is it?" A man's voice.

Brian cleared his throat. "You don't know us," he said loudly. "We're renting the cottage down the road from you—they call it Fern Cottage. We were driving home and we hit a deer. The deer ran onto your property. I think it might be badly hurt—maybe a broken leg."

There was a brief silence. Then, "A deer, you say? Its leg broke?"

"Yes. We think possibly."

"And what did you want me to do about it?"

Brian looked back at Delia. "Not a thing," he told the voice. "But we wanted you to know."

Now there was a longer silence. Delia left the car and stood beside Brian.

"What's happening?" she said.

"I guess nothing."

The speaker hummed. "Shut down your engine," the voice said. "I'll come to the gate."

*   *   *

THEY WAITED IN THE DARK for the embodiment of the voice to present itself.

"I'm scared," Delia said. "I hope it's the eccentric millionaire, and not the godfather."

Unexpectedly, the area inside the fence blazed into white light. Floodlights under the eaves of the house had come on, illuminating the night around the building. A couple of minutes later a man appeared. He opened one side of the gate and gestured them inside. With the light behind him he stood in patient silhouette; a holstered pistol was plainly visible at his left hip.

He played the beam of a flashlight over them, head to foot and up again to read their faces. Apparently satisfied by what he saw, he lowered the light.

"Come," he said, and when they obeyed he locked the gate after them. "I've seen no evidence of your injured animal. If she's truly in a bad way, God will do with her what he must."

He walked ahead, his shadow cast back to them. Details of man and house were obscure, though they could see that the man's hair was white, and at the house the windows were comforting yellow rectangles of lamplight. Off to the left was an open shed, slant-roofed, and under it they could make out the slatted grille of a white Jeep.

At the door the man paused. "Now you're here," he said, "you'll stay for a nightcap. We'll raise a solemn glass to your unlucky deer, be she dead or alive."

"That's generous of you," Brian said.

They followed into a long hallway, where their host found a switch that returned the world to midnight behind them. He un-buckled the belt of the holster and hung it from a peg on the wall beside other pegs that held coats, a couple of short jackets, assorted caps and hats and a pair of black binoculars suspended from a worn leather strap.

"Come," he said.

He opened the door into a lighted room—the room with the reassuring windows—and ushered them inside. In this normal at-mosphere the man became accessible: average height, ruddy-faced and clean-shaven, with a head of close-cropped white hair. A thin mouth; ice-blue eyes. Brian put him in his late sixties, an elderly man who clearly took proper care of himself, heavyset but not over-weight.

The man offered a large blunt-fingered hand. "Kerry Monaghan," he said. "I thought it best to defer the civilities until we'd achieved a civilized setting."

Brian shook Monaghan's hand. "Brian Varney," he said. "This is Delia."

"A pleasure," Monaghan said. "Beauty is ever welcome."

"Thank you," Delia said.

"Please." Their host indicated a sofa and several chairs both pillowed and caned. The spacious room featured a fireplace and a large Oriental carpet over a pine-board floor. On the fireplace mantel were photographs, and on end tables and a long, low coffee table a variety of magazines and pamphlets. "Be easy," Monaghan said. "I'll look to see what's in the drinks cupboard."

The two of them took to the sofa while their host disappeared into the hallway.

"He's hospitable," Brian said.

"Not what you'd expect from somebody who carries a gun."

"Eccentric," Brian said. "It's your word."

They looked around. Under the windows was a low bookcase, its shelves occupied by thin volumes in dull dust jackets. At the opposite end of the room stood a small square table with chess pieces set up as if a game were in progress.

"At least he plays chess," Brian said.

"So he can't be all bad?"

"Something like that." He picked a magazine off the coffee table and leafed through it.

"He certainly isn't interested in the injured deer," Delia said. "Which is why you've got us here."

"You heard him. God disposes."

"If any." She stretched and wandered behind the sofa to look at the photographs displayed on the mantel. She stopped at one, leaned to study it.

"Oh, my goodness," she said. "He's a priest."

"He's what?" Brian joined her.

"He's much, much younger," she said. She turned the picture toward him. "See here? A Catholic priest."

* * *

WHEN MONAGHAN RETURNED he was carrying a wooden tray laden with bottles and cordial glasses. He set the tray before his guests, pushing the stack of magazines aside.

"There's Baileys for the lady," he said, "or a little Drambuie from the top shelf. For the gentleman, brandy, or perhaps my own guilty favorite, grappa."

"I've never tried that," Brian said.

"I was introduced to it on a long-ago visit to Rome. I'm told it's a distillation from the fermented pulp left behind in wine-making." Monaghan poured two grappas and a Baileys. "I rarely take stronger drink than wine," he said. "This seems an occasion."

"But not a happy one," Delia said. "Nobody seems to give two hoots about that poor hurt deer."

Monaghan, who had already taken a seat across from the two of them, set his glass aside. He looked over at Brian, then back to Delia. He slapped his knees and stood up.

"Well then," he said, "let's have a serious look round." He waited for Brian to follow his lead. "For the sake of the lady, who will excuse us."

"I'll come with you," Delia said.

"No, no. We'll not be long," Monaghan told her. "It's little enough territory to be covered."

In the hall, Brian waited for his host to buckle the pistol belt and switch on the outside floods. Monaghan took two heavy flashlights from a cupboard under the coats and handed one to Brian. Then the two men descended the front steps and walked toward the gate.

"Delia can be abrupt," Brian said. "She likes things to be resolved."

"No need for apology." Monaghan stopped and rested his hand on Brian's shoulder. "Now you see: here's a beaten path just within the fence line. It goes full circle. If you follow it that way, and I this, we'll meet somewhere farthest from the gate. Keep playing your torch into the growth. If you see your damaged deer, give us a call out."

"Right," Brian said, and moved dutifully to his left. Monaghan went right, the beam of his flashlight flickering across the undergrowth of fern and gorse.

Brian's hope was to find nothing—no blood, no track, no sign of the animal he had hit. Ignorance is bliss, he would tell Delia. If we don't know what happened to the deer, we can assume it survived. Still, he played the flashlight as deeply as he could into the wilderness of Monaghan's immense backyard. The light discovered nothing, and after walking a couple of hundred feet along the fencing he grew increasingly optimistic.

But then he heard a gunshot—or something very much as he imagined a gunshot would sound—and the noise arrested him in his tracks. For a moment the world was echo, and then came a second shot. This time he was certain of what he had heard, and he began trotting alongside the fence toward it.

He called as he ran: "Monaghan! Mr. Monaghan!"

"Over here," came Monaghan's voice.

Their flashlight beams met. Monaghan stood at the edge of the brush, his pistol—square and black, enormous to Brian's eye—in his right hand. He swung the light of his torch into the wild green vegetation and Brian saw the deer, now dead.

"I smelled her before I saw her," Monaghan said. "Blood. The reek of it. You can see for yourself: the bone at its break pokes clean through the flesh. It's wondrous amazing she was able to clear my fence after your motorcar struck her."

"You killed it," Brian said. His tone was matter-of-fact, but was there truly an odor, and was it of blood—a humid sweetness heavy on the night air around them? The vegetation under the animal's shattered leg glistened magenta in the light. Two nearly bloodless bullet holes showed the way to its heart.

"Took her out of her misery. She was trying to stand, her breathing hoarse as death itself." Monaghan holstered the pistol. "There was nothing else for it."

"Delia will be devastated."

"She'll need to be reminded the death of an animal is not like some human death. They're ignorant, soulless creatures—poor things. They've neither premonition nor salvation."

*　*　*

In the end, Delia was allowed a glass of brandy.

"One good thing," Monaghan said. "It was indeed a doe—as I'd guessed from the way you two described it—but she wasn't pregnant." He shook his head and sighed. "If she'd been carrying a life, that would have been a dilemma. You know the glorious small poem, the one by your American poet, Stafford? It considers such a circumstance, and weighs the greater good."

"'Traveling Through the Dark,'" Delia said. "I make my students read it."

"Just so." Monaghan leaned toward his decanter. "Another touch of the brandy?"

"No, thank you."

"And nothing more for me," Brian said.

Monaghan sat back and folded his hands across his lap. "It's been quite the night," he said. "It's exceedingly rare for me to have visitors in this house. Indeed, you two are the first."

"Do you like living alone?" Delia asked. "Don't you start talking to yourself?"

"And what better company?" Monaghan said. Then, serious: "It's not entirely choice, but I've got accustomed to the sometime boredom of it. I have my reading, and I do have e-mail for contact with the outside universe. I play chess by computer besides, against various adversaries around the globe. Some matches occupy months."

"Chess is one of our rainy-day pastimes," Brian said.

"Is that a fact?"

"Brian has a pocket chess set," Delia said. "With little magnetic pieces."

"Then oughtn't we to have a game?" Monaghan cocked his head, one eyebrow raised. "I'd welcome a flesh and blood opponent. Which of you shall it be?"

"Brian," Delia said.

"I'm not very good," Brian said.

"We'll see about that." Monaghan put down his glass and stood up. "Let me first arrange for disposing of our poor dead animal."

* * *

FROM THE FRONT HALL THEY HEARD the flutter of a rotary-dial telephone. Monaghan moved as he talked, the movements changing the quality of light and shadow in the doorway.

"Mrs. Daly," they heard him say, "is your Micheal at home?"

Apparently Micheal was not, for Monaghan went on almost at once. "Well that's as should be," he said. "Would you pass a message on to him? Would you say that a fine red doe has had the misfortune to be struck by a motorcar nearby and badly crippled. Tell him I've just now put her out of her misery and she lies dead not fifty feet from my back door. I've no way to dress the creature myself, but Micheal is welcome to her if he'll come and haul her away. At the least he'll have a fine head for mounting. Will you tell him that?"

"It's nothing but a trophy to him," Delia said grimly.

"Hush," Brian said. "He'll hear."

"Let him."

"I thank you, Mrs. Daly. I'll look forward to at last meeting your Micheal face-to-face."

The phone dropped into its cradle and the hall light went out. Monaghan came back into the room.

"Now," he said, rubbing his hands together, "shall we have our match?"

He went to the game table and carried it forward, setting it in the space between Brian and himself. He began rearranging the chess pieces.

"This was but one contest of several I'm presently engaged in, with Micheal and others," Monaghan said. "It's kept in my head—though should the head fail, it's safely on the computer drive."

"Now I know I'm out of my depth," Brian said.

"What a gorgeous chess table," Delia said.

"Mahogany," Monaghan told her. "Inlaid with squares of ebony wood and ivory. I'm told it once belonged to Alekhine, and when that master died it was appropriated by a mourner who displayed a fierce good taste."

"Quite a history," Brian said.

"The little I know of it. The balance of its provenance is shrouded in the mists. It came to me by way of an Ulster bureaucrat, now deceased."

Monaghan took up two pawns and for a moment dropped his hands below table level. He held both fists out to Brian. "Choose."

Brian touched the back of Monaghan's right hand. "They must be very close friends of yours," he said, "the Dalys—if you can phone them at one o'clock in the morning."

Monaghan unclenched his hand to show the white pawn. "You could put it that way," he said.

Brian pushed his king's pawn. "I'm sorry. I couldn't help overhearing," he said.

"Oh, no mind," Monaghan said. "My acquaintance with Micheal and Clare Daly is what you might call fortuitous. They own the pub just where this road of ours meets the highway."

"We know it well," Brian said. In his mind's eye he could see the Dalys, the wife tall and full-bosomed, her large hands suggesting an impressive strength. She was in her forties, Brian had guessed, stiff black hair shot through with slivers of white. The husband—Micheal—was about the same age, but slighter, subdued. While his wife drew the ales and bantered with patrons, Micheal stayed in the shadows between counter and kitchen, alert and ready to be useful but not putting himself forward. He had a wariness about him, his eyes bright and their movement restless. "And we know the Dalys—though not by name until now."

"We call the place 'our local,'" Delia said.

"Well then—I came to this house nearly two years ago," Monaghan said. "Micheal bought the pub barely a month later, so in a manner of speaking we were strangers here together, both down from the North, both feeling our way amongst the natives, seeking respite from the madness left behind. What's odd is that we've never truly met one another. We play chess, as you saw. We communicate by phone or e-mail. Tomorrow will be our first encounter."

"You're actually a priest," Brian said. Intended as a question, the words came out like a statement, and for a moment Monaghan seemed taken aback.

"Ah," he said. "The photograph on the mantel." He leaned over the chess board. "It was the day of my ordination. I've too much sentiment in me not to commemorate it, the picture being one of the few reminders of what I was."

"You left the Church?" Delia said.

"Left the priesthood," Monaghan corrected. "It's now thirty years. It was at a time when the voice of God seemed less persuasive than

14

the voices I was hearing in the confessional." He paused, moved a piece forward. "And in the streets as well," he said. "It was for me a change of life as great as the first, but a different faith—a crusade, you might say. I'm retired from that as well."

"Regrets?" Brian asked.

"I rarely ask myself such questions. If thirty years ago you had told me that at the age of seventy-one I should still be carrying a loaded pistol, I'd have chided you for too little faith. It only proves, I suppose, that the politics we marry, and the violence we condone, finally change nothing."

Monaghan studied Brian's game, his expression skeptical. "This is a curious deployment of your forces," he said. "Curious and obscure."

"I count on my ignorance," Brian said. "I figure that if I don't know what I'm doing, neither will the opponent."

"I had comrades who similarly followed instinct. Most are dead." He smiled and winked at Delia. "Gamesmanship," he told her.

"Do you and Micheal talk about the future? Of the North, I mean—of a united Ireland someday?"

Monaghan shook his head. "We shy away, we two, from such speculation. It was not easy for me to be open with Micheal, nor he with me, and even now we confine our messages to matters of a mundane sort. Micheal appears to be a master of many trades, and so our association has concerned itself with the everydays of landscape and mechanics. It was Micheal who persuaded me to paint my gate its gaudy orange, though it was no favorite color of mine. He won me over with the argument of economy: he called one day to tell me he'd got a grand paint bargain from a shop in Tralee; what a waste, he argued, not to take advantage. A demon of persuasion, Micheal is."

"It catches the eye," Delia said.

"And do you have connections to Ireland yourself?" Monaghan asked.

"So I'm told," Brian said. "My father's grandfather is supposed to have come from Kinsale. That must have been in the mid-nineteenth century."

"Then you're here to look him up."

"I haven't yet," Brian said. "We went through Kinsale on a Sunday."

"We might go back there," Delia said. "But time's getting short."

"That's my part of the world, as happens," Monaghan said. "Born in Youghal. Sent up to seminary in Dublin when I came of age. And then continued my vocation northward."

"There was a news report this noon about a shooting near Belfast," Brian said. "Somebody gunned down by a man on a motorbike."

"True," Monaghan said. He placed a pawn. "Red Hand. Protestants with a proven taste for murder."

"So insane," Delia said. "So pointless."

Monaghan smiled. "My mother had a saying: 'If God had meant us to be English, he'd not have thought up the Irish Sea.' Thus do mothers marry geography and politics."

"You push your differences so far back in time," Delia said. "You Irish."

"Well we have memories, don't you see, and the roots reach far and deep down—past Cromwell himself. The Irish have elephant brains, I think."

He studied Brian's moves all the time he talked, countering, watching, countering. His game was not mechanical, but swifter and surer. He talked, but his eyes and his focus never left the board. Now he rubbed his chin and slid a rook forward. "Mate," he said.

Brian's shoulders slumped. He toppled his king on its side and pushed his chair away from the board. "I guess my famous ignorance has failed me."

"We'll see," Monaghan said. "Shall we have another?"

"It's terribly late," Delia said.

Brian looked at her.

"We have plans for tomorrow," she said. "We're driving to Ennis."

"It's a journey easy and short enough," Monaghan said. "Why not tomorrow then? No matter how late."

"We'll try," Brian said. "I can't promise."

"Done." Monaghan stood, right hand extended to them. Brian shook the hand; Delia appeared not to notice it.

"You've been kind," she said. "But I'm sorry for the reason we met."

"Ah, the unfortunate animal." Monaghan moved the chess table back to its original place at the end of the room; in a matter of moments he reset it to the game he had wiped out earlier. "There's something to be said for necessity," he said. "Never mind whither our hearts may bend, often it's circumstance rules us."

*   *   *

Driving back from Ennis the next evening, they quarreled over Monaghan. The weather was changeable; they drove in and out of rain showers, great dark clouds boiling up out of the west to drench them, then giving way to amiable high blue sky. The car radio was playing; on the outskirts of Limerick a news broadcast commenced. It was all about the North: a cache of arms uncovered in Donegal; an inquiry into the use of force by the R.U.C.; the Red Hand claiming responsibility for yesterday's murder.

"You see?" Delia said. "He knew."

"An educated guess," Brian said.

"A certain knowledge."

And that was how the quarrel began. There was *something*, she said; politics or not, there was something sinister about the man. *Reclusive*, said Brian, is not necessarily *sinister*. But what about the gun, the electric fence, the security business? And was that his real name? Hadn't Brian noticed that *Kerry* and *Monaghan* were both names of Irish counties? Had he really been a priest?

"I don't trust him," she said. "Tell me the honest truth: Did you see it?"

"See what?"

"The deer. Did you actually see it?"

"Of course I saw it."

"Did you see it *before* he put it down?"

"No," Brian admitted. "It was already dead when I got to the spot."

"I think Monaghan's the kind of man who likes killing," Delia said. "Never mind all that malarkey about poetry and beauty and something not so strong for the lady."

"Delia—The deer was in agony. You could literally smell the blood. Monaghan did it a favor."

"I don't think of death as a 'favor,'" she said. "And I can't believe we're going back tonight for more chess. Monaghan *demolished* you in that game."

"But that was expected, wasn't it? I'm no chess whiz. I can't compete against a man who keeps multiple games in his head."

"Then we should drive straight to the cottage," Delia said. "Forget about another stupid game."

"I promised him," Brian said.

She closed her eyes, rested her head against the window. "Sometimes I don't understand you at all."

Brian concentrated on his driving—holding his arms uncomfortably rigid, as if he had not been driving on the left for weeks.

"How about a stop at our local?" he said. "A stiff nightcap for the lady."

Delia relented. "That's your first smart idea of the day."

But when they arrived at the pub it was closed, the parking lot empty of cars. Brian got out and tried the door, but it was locked; when he peered inside he saw no lights, no sign of life.

"Too bad," Delia said. "I've gotten to like this place."

"Never mind. Monaghan will break out the drinks."

"Watch my kibitzing," Delia said. "I plan to get drunk as a skunk."

* * *

FROM THE CREST OF THE LONG SLOPE where they had struck the deer the night before, they saw a single car parked at Monaghan's driveway. It was unusual for hikers to be out on the trails so late, and as they came nearer they saw that it was a police car—a white Gardai sedan. An officer wearing a lime-yellow vest was leaning against a fender.

"What's this?" Brian said.

He stopped alongside the Gardai car and rolled down his window. The officer, uniformed under his vest, a shiny-billed garrison cap pulled low on his forehead, leaned toward him.

"What's happening?" Brian asked.

"Nothing for yourselves to be concerned with, sir," the policeman said. "Official investigation."

"Investigating what? What's going on?"

Delia nudged him. Up by the orange gate a black Land Rover was parked. In its driver's seat was a man, apparently a soldier, and at the gate itself stood two more soldiers—all three in camouflage uniforms, black berets, black boots and belts. The two at the gate carried machine guns; one man had his weapon at the ready, the other held his loosely over one arm, the muzzle pointed toward the ground. The gate itself was shut; an enormous X, done in two broad black strokes, was painted across it.

The policeman had come closer, bending to look in at them. "You're American?"

"Yes."

"Might I see your passports, please?"

"Mine's at our cottage," Brian said. "I could get it; it's just down the road."

"I have mine," Delia said. She rummaged in her handbag, offered the passport to the officer, who examined it and returned it.

"We were invited to stop in for a game of chess," Brian said.

"I'm afraid there'll to be no matches tonight," the officer said.

"Are those soldiers?"

The policeman stepped away. "We're the police," he said, "not the army. Move along now. Death's happened here and we've work to do." He dismissed them with the back of his hand.

"Let's go," Delia murmured.

Brian put the car in gear and drove on. "What the hell," he said.

For the next few days, their last in Ireland, they of course made guesses about what had happened to the man who called himself Kerry Monaghan. Surely it had to do with the strife in the North, but what? There was nothing in the *Irish Times*, nothing in the *Examiner*, nothing on the RTE evening news programs to enlighten them.

"The policeman didn't say 'murder,' did he?"

Delia shook her head. "Death *happened*," she reminded him.

"He wasn't a young man," Brian said. "It might have been natural causes."

"Then why the police—the uniforms, all the guns? Use your head," she said. "And where is his friend Micheal?"

"What does that matter?"

"He chose the paint," she said. "He marked the place."

The Gardai vehicles did not appear again outside the disfigured orange gate, though for two days an armed policeman stood guard—a genuine sentry beside the imitation sentry-box—and by the third day he too was gone. The pub owned by the Dalys did not reopen.

During that time the weather turned magnificent: blue skies with billowy white clouds that scudded across the sun and cast restless shade on hill and valley. "The curse of the tourist," Brian said. "Everything turns perfect on the eve of departure."

Even the black-faced sheep—whose wool until now had shown a dingy yellow-gray, each animal marked with a blue dye-stroke of ownership—changed character. On the sunlit green hillsides they were brilliantly white, their coats pristine, unmarked.

"What's happened?" Delia said.

"They've been sheared," Brian said. "Or is it 'shorn'?"

"They're so brand-new," she said. "So clean and white, so small."

* * *

Home in Boston, Brian's relatives—uncles, aunts and cousins—wanted all the details of the trip, as if Ireland were homeland instead of a place to visit quite removed from dead ancestors. Yes, he'd gone to Kinsale. No, he hadn't looked up the great-grandparents, the hall where the records were kept being closed on Sunday. No, he and Delia had skipped Dublin; they had talked about taking the train up to Belfast, except that there was a flaring up of riots and bombings and an assassination that put them off. Perhaps next summer, or the summer after. And oh, here were crisp ten-pound notes carrying the picture of James Joyce, one for each of the relatives to keep because in January Ireland would convert to the euro.

What neither Brian nor Delia could explain to his relatives was how they had gone to Ireland partly in the hope of understanding its divisions, but had only confirmed the tourist ignorance they arrived with. That now it was an ignorance made flesh and blood by a former priest with an invented name was deadly important to themselves, but it could not have enlightened others.

On the way back from Ennis—that last day-trip of their Irish vacation—Delia had bought a pot of lavender at a garden shop in Limerick and set it on a windowsill of the rented cottage. She knew it was forbidden to take a plant out of the country, but while it was hers it freshened the place with a scent no less effective for all that it was a subtle one. The last morning, she broke off the blossoms, put them in an envelope and took them through Shannon security in her carry-on bag.

As for Brian, what he brought home to the States was the image of the doe, its injured leg soaked with blood, the stark femur splintered, protruding, the two entry wounds in the animal's breast like black holes in an obscure universe of death—and Monaghan, the author of this benevolent sacrifice, standing in torchlight, pistol still drawn. Long after he had broken with Delia, this was for Brian the perfect summing up of their holiday in Ireland: "Blood," the old priest had said. "The reek of it."

An Age of Beauty and Terror

It is a midweek evening; the restaurant called The Swan is not crowded. Thomas Madden and his wife, Edith, have been seated at a two-spot near a window—though it is after dark and nothing is to be seen through the glass—and are drinking their first martinis when Madden says, "Look."

Edith pauses, the martini glass at the level of her lower lip. "What?" she says.

"Look. There." Madden doesn't point. He tilts his head and lowers his left eyelid. His wife turns.

At a table in the corner farthest from the windows sits a middle-aged man—expensively dressed in a brown silk suit, an off-white shirt, brown tie with a plain gold pin—talking with the waitress. The waitress wears a long-skirted uniform, navy blue, with an open-neck white blouse. The man's hand is under the young woman's skirt; Madden has watched it from the moment it slipped under her hem, has traced its movement up the outside of her left thigh and around to her buttock, where it is now cupped indiscreetly, the skirt hiked up at the crook of the man's elbow.

"I don't see anything," Edith Madden says. "What am I supposed to be looking at?"

"His hand," Madden says in a hoarse whisper. "The man's naughty hand."

"Naughty?" His wife swivels in her seat, the cocktail glass still poised at the level where her mouth will be when she turns back to the table.

"His hand. Under the waitress's skirt. Up her leg."

Edith Madden studies the man and the waitress. "No," she says finally. "No, I don't think so."

Madden makes a noise of exasperation, like a seal or a tired horse. What is the matter with you women? he wants to blurt out, but catches himself in time. Instead he sips his own martini and watches the guilty pair over the rim of the glass. The middle-aged man—actually, he is probably only a few years older than Madden— is buttering a Parker House roll, holding half the roll in his left hand, buttering it with the knife in his right.

"He damned well was," Madden says.

"I think not," his wife insists. "Not in front of the whole world."

* * *

A DAY OR SO LATER, Madden leaves his office a few minutes before noon and strolls through a small, well-manicured park on his way to have lunch with a friend, a former colleague.

It is spring, early May, and all morning Madden has found it difficult to pay full attention to the work on his desk. He remarks to himself that he is usually not easily distracted from duty, and that he has a history of being indifferent to Nature—to the seasons, the changing pitches of sunlight, goldengroves unleaving and all that sort of thing. Yet here he is, crossing a park, noticing that the trees are budded and the grass has begun to recover from winterkill. He breathes the balmy air with a sense of real pleasure. Perhaps he is undergoing a change of life, taking a new lease, entering a second childhood. He will have to ask Dr. Himmel.

He is almost through the park; the wrought-iron fence that surrounds it is just ahead of him. Beyond the fence is the wide, much-trafficked street he will have to cross. He has in fact reached the gate, one hand on the coarse black rail of it, and has turned back to survey these unexpectedly attractive surroundings one last time before dealing with the traffic that lies between himself and the restaurant where his friend is waiting. And there he stops, his mouth open, his face amazed.

What arrests him is a young couple at the base of an elm tree near the center of the park. The elm is a relic, many of its branches cut off and the juncture of those branches painted in shiny black ovals, a cable holding two of its upper limbs from surrendering to gravity. The couple, a man and a woman, are engrossed in each other. They have all their limbs, and they are surrendering to gravity in the most obvious way. Madden is transfixed.

The young man is lying on his back in the shadow of the elm, the young woman bent over him, kissing him. As Madden watches—he cannot help himself—the woman unbuttons her blouse and strips it off. She is naked under the blouse, and her small breasts make her seem frail, intensely vulnerable. Again she bends over the young man. Her small, petal-colored nipples brush his lips, his tongue. She lifts her pretty face into sunlight, closes her eyes, presses the young man's face against her breasts.

Madden turns away. There are others in the park: small children with their mothers, men reading folded newspapers, a blond woman in glasses taking a deli-wrapped sandwich out of a brown paper bag. What is the world coming to?

After lunch ("What is the world coming to?" he has said to his friend) Madden retraces his path through the park. The couple is gone, the park is empty and colder. Over the bare, pruned branches of a rose bush someone has draped a flimsy white blouse. It resembles a crumpled scrap of waxed paper, something discarded by a picnicker too indifferent to look for a rubbish barrel.

*   *   *

"WHAT AM I SUPPOSED TO TELL YOU?" Dr. Himmel says. "That you're having hallucinations? That the world is not as you perceive it? That you're going crazy?"

"Is that what's happening?" Madden says. "Am I going crazy?"

"Girl crazy," the doctor says. "Woman crazy." He crosses his legs and lights a cigarette, even though Madden has asked several times in the last five years that Himmel not smoke in his presence. "I ask you, Thomas, who knows you better than I do? Inside out, outside in, from the womb of your angel mother to the deathbed of your prick of a father—I ask you: Do I know you?"

"You know me," Madden admits.

"So trust me when I tell you this has nothing to do with clinical crazy."

"Then what?"

"Desire," the doctor says. He blows smoke toward the brown drapes at the windows, studying it as if desire itself were a thin blue cloud swirling in sunlight. "Desire, guilt, the misgivings of a man who maybe can't get it up so easily or so often as he used to, nostalgia for vanished youth. You name it, Thomas. Make me a list."

Madden sighs and sneezes. He is hearing abstractions. What Himmel is confessing is his ignorance: Madden may not know what's happening, but neither does the doctor.

"Suppose they're hallucinations," he says. "Suppose I am seeing things that aren't real. What should I do?"

"A little invented voyeurism," the doctor says. "How could it hurt?"

"It frightens me. I want it to stop."

Himmel shrugs and rolls the cigarette between his thumb and

26

ring finger. "Count your blessings," he says. "Enjoy the free enter-tainment your mind is giving you. Not even a cover charge."

"But it's all too real," Madden says. "I should have picked that blouse off the rosebush. I should have brought it to you."

The doctor sighs. "Your view of the female is essentially a contra-diction," he says. "You believe every woman is so innocent, you can-not imagine a man doing to her the things you tell me you see. At the very same time, you are yourself so naïve that you believe the woman will accept without protest—will welcome—any indignity the man visits upon her."

"Do I?" Madden says.

"Do you not?" Dr. Himmel stubs his cigarette into the ash-tray. "You must begin to explain yourself to yourself." He consults his watch. "But not today. Next Monday; then begin."

Madden hesitates. "Am I addicted to sex?" he asks.

Himmel pats Madden's upper arm and steers him toward the of-fice door. "You're a man on the edge of middle age," he says, "the prime of life. You should ask yourself this question: How can a nor-mal urge be addictive?"

* * *

IN THE SAME RESTAURANT where Madden and his wife disagreed about what was being done to a waitress, the waitress herself ap-pears at Madden's table.

"Let me tell you our specials," she says. "The catch of the day is red snapper. The quiche is Lorraine. The soup is Wisconsin cheese." She reaches to fill his water glass; her breasts are provocative, Mad-den thinks, trying not to peer into the generous opening of her uni-form shirt. A small rectangle of plastic alongside the opening reads *Halina*.

Madden notes that Halina is dark and remarkably tall. She is short-waisted, full-bosomed; her height is in the wonderfully long legs hidden beneath her ankle-length skirt. She stands within his easy reach, the sweating pitcher cradled between her pale, thin-fingered hands.

"May I get you something from the bar?" she says.

"You may," Madden says. "A very dry martini, up, with a twist."

"That's nice," Halina says. "Why don't you let me bring something else up with a twist?" She winks at Madden.

"I beg your pardon?"

"Sorry," Halina says. "I was repeating your order out loud. It's a bad habit of mine."

"That's quite all right," he says. He feels a cool tickle of perspiration down his sides, hears a buzzing in his ears.

"You look at the menu," the waitress says. "I'll slip into a dry martini."

"Thank you," Madden says. While he reads the menu, he remembers what the doctor has been saying about hallucinations. He especially remembers "What harm can it do?"

He begins to relax. The martini will help. Beyond the hostess's desk, Halina has gone behind the bar to chat with the young bartender while he mixes Madden's drink. The two are laughing, and their laughter makes Madden happy; he feels he is a part of their conversation, a confidant, an equal. The bartender pours the martini and dumps the ice into a sink under the counter; he cuts a yellow ribbon of lemon peel into the stemmed glass; he plucks a green olive from behind the counter and drops it between Halina's breasts. Madden can hear her surprised exclamation, sees her clutch at the hollow where the olive has disappeared. Then she giggles. The bartender shows her a tiny cocktail onion, then deftly pitches it in after the olive. Next is a maraschino cherry.

"*Two* cherries there," Madden calls out from his table. "For sym-

28

metry." He is proud of the ease with which he has caught the spirit of the evening.

Halina is startled, and turns, perplexed, to look at him. The bartender sets the martini on a round tray, and Halina delivers it to Madden's table.

"You asked for a twist," she reminds him.

"I'll say." Madden takes the martini, sips from it; the drink is watery. When the waitress turns to carry the tray back to the bar, he puts out his arm to block her way, his hand making contact with her plump bottom.

The expression on Halina's face changes from accommodation to disgust. She looks, coldly, at his arm.

"Move it," she says, "or I'll break it."

*   *   *

"You should get out of town for a while," Dr. Himmel says. "Go on a trip. Take the wife and make it into a second honeymoon."

"But what's happening to me?" Madden says.

"What do you think is happening?"

"I don't know. I seem to be turning into some kind of sex maniac. Everything I look at becomes suggestive, sexual, erotic."

"So, how do you feel about that?" Himmel says through the haze of cigarette smoke.

Madden ponders. "Helpless," he says. "Out of control."

The doctor nods and contemplates the ceiling.

"If it's the free entertainment you say it is, why can't I enjoy it? Why do things always end badly?"

"How 'badly'?"

"Unpleasantly. They depress me."

"What do you think is the answer to your question?"

"I have no idea."

"Then take some time," the doctor says. "Think about it. Seriously—go somewhere for a nice holiday."

"But isn't that running away from the problem?"

"You're already running away. Ask yourself a couple of questions: 'Why isn't some of this stuff happening to me? How come it's always the other guy who gets to feel the woman up, who bites her pert little nipples, who plays kid games in her cleavage?'"

Madden wonders if Himmel is going too far. "Are you saying I can only enjoy sex vicariously?"

"Vicariously," Himmel echoes. "You said it, not me. Take that trip. Find some unfamiliar scenery, places you've never been. Rest. Unwind." The doctor leans forward, points a plump finger at him. "Listen to me, Thomas: life is not a dirty movie."

"Are you telling me I'm projecting?" Madden says.

* * *

"I'm going out to the pool," Edith Madden says. "Are you coming?"

"I'd rather read." Madden is propped against three pillows on the telephone side of the king-sized bed. This is in a Holiday Inn north of Boston, where the Maddens have already spent one night and plan to spend one more before driving on for a few days in Montreal. "You go enjoy yourself."

But after his wife has left the room, Madden decides he would rather not be alone with the novel he is reading and changes his mind. He puts on black swim trunks and a white robe, slides his feet into his sandals, and strolls down the narrow hallway to the pool. The longer he walks, the warmer and moister the atmosphere becomes, until the air around him is steamy and reeks of pungent chlorine. Stepping into the domed pool area, he sheds his robe and lays it beside a chaise longue; then he flops down onto the chaise and sighs. Himmel is right; unwinding is exactly what he needs.

He leans down to draw the paperback out of the pocket of the robe and takes a good look around. A restaurant skirts one side of the pool area, a tiny bar is located opposite; not far away, tastefully half-concealed by potted palms, are pinball machines and video games. The adult pool is a straightforward rectangle, and not far from one end of it is a child's wading pool, small and round. Together, the two pools look like a green exclamation point outlined in white tile. Edith is in the center of the larger, doing a leisurely backstroke. Beyond her, two young women are tossing a water-polo ball back and forth. Madden catches his wife's eye and waves. Then he settles back and opens the novel.

He has scarcely started reading when a small commotion distracts him: the two young women—both brunette, one in a red bikini, the other in a yellow—have given up playing catch and begun to shriek and splash water on each other. Madden thinks they are rather too noisy; it is as if they are trying to call attention to themselves, but when he looks around he doesn't see any young men worthy of their interest.

He returns to his book. Edith pulls herself out of the pool and stands over him as she towels her wet hair.

"Are you going in?" she says. "You should probably get your goggles; they seem to use a lot of chemical stuff in the water."

"I thought I'd try and get through this," Madden says.

Edith tilts her head and reads the book's cover. "I'd have thought you'd be finished with Chandler by now."

"I keep re-reading. He's good."

"I wish I could get you interested in Simenon."

Madden shrugs. "He's French," he says.

"What's wrong with the French?" She drags a beach chair over and sits beside him.

"Nothing," he says. He puts the book face down against his chest and glances across the pool. He doesn't know when it happened, but the two pretty women are naked—their bikinis are tiny blobs of color near the end of the diving board—and they have begun making love in the center of the pool. Madden watches them, memorizing them so that he can give Dr. Himmel explicit details. They kissed, he will say. They touched breasts against breasts. They lay in the water face to belly, belly to face. Then they made a living water wheel, revolving while they devoured each other: bare backs and plump buttocks and flowing dark hair, like dolphin shapes in the turbulent pool.

When they have climbed out of the pool and gone away, Madden lies back, enervated, drained.

"Did you see all that?" he asks.

"See what?" his wife answers. She has slid down in the cloth seat, her neck resting on the chair back, her arms folded over her stomach. Her legs still wear water beads that shine on her skin like small diamonds.

"Nothing." He sits upright with an effort. "Why don't we go back to the room?"

"After a while. I'm feeling wonderfully relaxed."

"Maybe. . . I could relax you a bit more." He puts a hand out to his wife. With a tentative forefinger he touches a water droplet on the inside of one thigh, close to the vee of her swimsuit.

Edith turns her head lazily and half opens her eyes.

"Oh, Thomas," she says. "Act your age."

*   *   *

SUNDAY NIGHT HE AND HIS WIFE are back home, and the next morning, standing before the bathroom mirror to shave, Madden experiences a wicked anxiety attack. Such attacks are rare in his life, and this one is of an unusual violence; he wants to scream, like a man suffering physical pain. He drops his razor into the sink and hammers both fists against his stomach, as if he could by force obliterate the fear that churns there. He rummages through the medicine chest, hoping to find a few tranquilizers left over from years ago, but of course his wife, as a precaution, throws away all leftover prescriptions. A precaution against what? he wonders, and he thinks a stale Valium would be as useful now as a fresh one. He knows that, ethically, no doctor can prescribe a tranquilizer over the telephone; fortunately, Monday is Madden's regular appointment day—at two o'clock. If he can make it through the morning, somehow Himmel will rescue him.

He arrives in the waiting room twenty minutes early, even though he is aware that Himmel generally runs behind schedule. Madden has in fact had a terrible day, reduced at one point to perching on the edge of his desk chair at work, hugging himself—his hands gripping his arms so hard that he imagines he will find black-and-blue finger marks when he goes to bed tonight—and shaking uncontrollably. He has gone to The Swan for lunch, but wasn't able to eat. He has sat in the Public Gardens for a half-hour, hoping Nature might soothe him, but the anxiety held a firm grip on the scruff of his mind. Now he sorts through the stacks of old magazines, hoping to find one of recent vintage that will carry him up to the moment of asking the doctor to write him a prescription. He manages to find an issue of *People* that is barely two months old and settles himself at one end of a scuffed leather couch.

He has scarcely begun to turn pages when the hall door opens and a strikingly lovely woman enters. She reports to the receptionist, hangs her fur jacket in the corner, and sits at the other end of his couch. Madden studies her, obliquely, pretending to read the tattered magazine in his lap. She is in her early thirties, he thinks; her hair is reddish-brown, her skin pale; she uses very little makeup. She is dressed in casual good taste: a soft blue cardigan worn over a plain blouse, a gray corduroy skirt, short-heeled black shoes. Is she bare-legged? She seems to be.

After a few minutes, Madden is aware that she is sizing him up, though she is much more direct about it than he has been. She is, after all, not pretending to read an out-of-date magazine. Instead, she has nested herself in the corner of the couch, folded her arms, and chosen to stare at him. Madden feels himself blushing. Why? he asks himself. Because she is an attractive woman, he answers, and I am embarrassed and perplexed by her attention.

"I haven't seen *you* before," the woman says.

He acts surprised, pretends that he has just now realized he is not alone, even though the waiting room contains a number of men and women—not to mention several children—waiting to be counseled by other doctors and by the clinic's family psychologists.

"Are you a regular?" she says.

He smiles. "I don't think people come here if they're 'regular.' I think all of us are 'irregular,' if you see what I mean."

She cocks her head. "I see," she says. "What's your hang-up?"

The question startles him, and he can't think of a fast response.

"Sex, probably." She says it for him. "I saw you giving me the once-over, trying not to be obvious."

"I don't think. . . ," Madden begins.

"It's all right," she says. "Me too."

Madden looks at her. She crosses her legs so that he is able to see a considerable field of white thigh under her skirt. Oh, God, he thinks, is it starting again? He takes a quick look at his watch. How near is his appointment? How late is Himmel today?

"I have this thing about men," the woman says. "This compulsion."

"Is that so?" Madden says. He says it coolly, but he makes a rapid survey of the room. All the adults are absorbed in dog-eared reading matter; the children—three of them—are playing with toy cars at the edge of the carpet.

The woman slides down the couch toward him. "Are you gay?"

"No," Madden says. "Not at all."

The woman slides closer and takes his magazine away from him. "I know plenty about men. What they like. What they don't." She rumples his hair. "Come to think of it," she says, "what's wrong with wanting every man I see?"

"It's promiscuous," Madden says.

The woman loosens his necktie, nibbles at his earlobe. His mind spins downward in the whirlpool of her exotic perfume.

"There's 'promise' in 'promiscuity,'" she says.

By now she is all over him, and Madden cannot help being excited. When she kisses him, her delicate tongue dancing in his mouth like a lascivious hummingbird, he hears himself moan; when she clutches at him, he pushes himself against her small, hot hand.

"Think about it," she says hoarsely.

She has unbelted him; her slender hand and wrist are gliding over him like an inquisitive long-necked animal. Madden realizes that his own hands are moving in a frenzy under the woman's skirt, that he is actually tearing at her blouse buttons with his teeth. What good is Himmel? he wonders. When the woman straddles him, he hurls himself upward with such force that the two of them topple onto the floor.

At this moment the doctor emerges from his office to discover the two of them. Himmel takes in the scene and claps his hands.

"Bravo, Thomas!" he cries. "Bravo!"

Thomas wonders how he should respond. In the meantime, the other adult clients wait quietly for their appointments, while their children say "Vrumm! Vrumm!" and rub toy cars against the carpet to make the tiny wheels spin and whirr.

Charm

The Maurice Ducharme School is a three-story brick building at the corner of Thompson and Nason streets in Scoggin, Maine. The brick is of two colors, sand-beige accented with scarlet in a stepped pattern at the building's four corners and around the weathered-oak entrance doors. The walks in front of Ducharme are of WPA cement, with occasional squares of newer, raw white stuff. The school was built in the early nineteen-thirties—nearly sixty years ago—and has had no updating except for a new roof after the 1938 hurricane. It houses all twelve grades of the town's Catholic school children. It also houses, at the basement level, the St. Ignatius Church, one of two Catholic churches in the town, the other being Holy Family, on the west side of the river. Few of Scoggin's Catholic families send their children to the public schools; they expect the nuns to do the teaching at least through middle school, ten years when the girl pupils are still required to wear the white blouse and navy-blue jumper uniform, and the boys are restricted to dark trousers, white shirts, and neckties. Even after ninth grade, only the more liberal Catholics turn to the public high school to prepare their teens for college.

Most of the townspeople, but especially the Protestants, refer to Ducharme as "the parochial school"; the children who attend it sometimes call it, not always sarcastically, "the charm school."

* * *

PETER GOODWIN IS HIMSELF a lapsed Catholic, but he has taught senior high English literature and creative composition at Ducharme for a dozen years. At Fordham, in the nineteen-sixties, he had intended to major in philosophy, but in all the upheavals of the age—the war, the peace movement, the licentiousness of soul and body that swept over American campuses—he dropped out, married a Unitarian from Schenectady, and eventually came home to Maine. He got a teaching degree, secondary, English and Language Arts, from the college at Farmington, spent four years in a rural junior high near Bangor and eight years at Coney High in Augusta, and finally—he and his wife, Shelley, having acquired along the way three children and a rusty Subaru—moved to Scoggin and the Ducharme school. This, he likes to tell their friends, was in the first year of the Reagan regime, A.D.—*After Democrats.*

Peter is forty-eight; his youngest child, the daughter, Jackie, will graduate from Bradford in May; the two boys, Tim and Vance, are both in sales in Boston. Shelley, four years Peter's junior, runs a bookstore that specializes in children's literature. Sometimes Peter finds himself, idly, assessing these facts of his life. He reviews the turns that have brought him to this former mill town—the textile and shoe factories moved South in the nineteen-fifties—and ensconced him in a school run by a Church whose faith he renounced long ago, though "renounced" seems, even to Peter, to put the matter too strongly.

When he tries nowadays to focus his mind on his loss of faith, he imagines New York City is to blame—that it was the City, with its aura of infinite temptation, that paganized him and made God seem unnecessary. Wherever the blame, Peter's renunciation endures: St.

Ignatius Church is directly below him; he has never descended to it, never knelt before its altar, never entered its confessional. The priests, Father Devon and his assistant, Father Guillaume, are acquaintances—Peter nods to them in the school corridors, they drink sweet punch together on Parents' Night—but the three of them are neither friends nor adversaries. Day after day Peter is surrounded in his work by nuns and brothers, by women and men in black devoted to God and His Work, by children whose anxious concern is to be catechized and found worthy, by artifacts and icons and images that glorify Salvation and the Saviour. Peter is unmoved and uncontrite. The Deity is all but forgotten; He is not where Peter's life is centered.

* * *

THAT CENTER—THAT STILL POINT around which, like feral animals just beyond the firelight, Peter's concerns make a restless circling—is Woman. The word is not plural, never *women*. Peter is not unhappy in his marriage; carnal novelty does not tempt him. Even in his forties, he is not suffering midlife crisis. Though he may be without faith, at least he is not unfaithful. Simply, it is Woman, capitalized and abstracted and ideal, that holds him like a planet caught in regular orbit around a steadfast, unreachable star.

The day he arrived at Ducharme, it was one of the sisters who captured him: Mary Martha—Sisters of Charity, BVM—a black-cloaked, white-cowled nun, her forehead pale and unlined, eyes brown and fawn-trusting, lips innocent of rouge. She and Peter sat side by side at student desks in the fifth-grade classroom, gathered with a half-dozen others for the rituals of new-teacher orientation. The principal, Sister Florence, conducted them through the forms for medical insurance, for keys to the outer doors, for income-tax withholding, for diocesan files. When the principal began her formal welcoming speech, Peter leaned toward Sister Mary Martha, partly to read her name from the top of one of the forms, partly to ask, *sotto voce*, "What do you teach?" Her brown eyes met his coolly. "Ninth-grade English," she said. "What about you?" "Also English," he whispered. "Senior high." That they shared a common subject matter pleased him and made him feel less a stranger in this unaccustomed environment. Perhaps he and Sister Mary Martha would be friends; she looked nothing like the desiccated nuns of his growing up in Portland, of the overcrowded grammar school, of sports-mad Cheverus High School during the thousand days of a Catholic President, and though today she wore the habit, he knew that in these modern times she was not bound to that uniform. He wondered about her appearance in street clothes—how feminine she would seem, what vanity she might betray. So absorbed was he in the woman beyond the veil that he scarcely attended to Sister Florence's orientation lecture, and when it was time for questions he directed his to Sister Mary Martha.

"But who *is* Maurice Ducharme?" he whispered.

"I think he was a lay brother in the local diocese," she whispered back. "Didn't Sister say so? Early in this century—maybe before World War I. He did something heroic and holy, or had a vision, or made a pronouncement that found God's favor."

Peter nodded. "I see," he said.

Sister Mary Martha gave him a gentle nudge with her cloaked elbow. "You know how these things happen," she said. "It's just a trick of being in the right place at the right time."

"Like the Virgin," he said.

Her brown eyes widened in surprise, and then, trying not to laugh, she put both hands to her face and snorted. When she had regained her composure, she was blushing; the heightened color on her brow made the white of her cowl seem to glow, as if from inner light.

"Shame on you," she whispered. "Shame, shame, shame." But she was smiling, and Peter was entranced.

*   *   *

SISTER MARY MARTHA WRITES POETRY. Some afternoons when Peter comes into the school library he finds her bowed over sheets of scrap paper—the back sides of hektographed diocesan attendance reports or blank computer forms daubed with the red ink that warns of the end of the box—and he knows she is immersed in a poem. Now that they have been friends for so long a time, he isn't afraid to be critical of her creative work, but early on, when he was feeling his way with her, he consciously held back his judgments—tempered them, made them as gentle and tentative as he knew how. Often he pleaded ignorance: "I don't understand this image; educate me." Then she was eager to explain and, if he was lucky, in the course of the explanation she would discover the imprecision he had been bothered by. "What a good teacher you are," she would say. "How fortunate your students are to have the gift of you."

Over time Peter has come to know Sister Mary Martha as well as he knows any of his other friends, and each piece of the jigsaw puzzle that comprises her life has surprised him by its banality—as if a nun could not have grown up like other women, or as if her decision to marry Christ ought to have transformed her mundane girlhood, retroactively, into an exemplary devotional apprenticeship. The truth is, Sister has said, that her early life was ordinary as pie and ice cream.

"Except that Daddy was older than most of my friends' fathers." She told him this, late one afternoon over stale coffee in the Maurice Ducharme cafeteria. "He was in his forties when he married my mother. I think having a daughter was a surprise to him; there was always a peculiar distance between us, as if he didn't know how to express his feelings toward me."

"And your mother?"

"Ordinary, quiet, what they used to call 'a homemaker.' She sang in the choir and belonged to Sodality and worked for the bake sales. Pushed Daddy to go to morning mass. I adored her, wanted to *be* her. I must have been the perfect Catholic child. I even made her put extra starch in my blouses." Sister Mary Martha smiled across the table—not at Peter, but at the image of the schoolgirl self she had been. "There are snapshots," she said. "Mousy but neat."

"Then what?"

"The usual. Upper-middle of my high school class. Secretarial school in Boston. A job in the advertising department at Jordan Marsh, carrying proofs around, running artwork to the engraver's. I liked it."

"But not enough."

"Oh, you know. A man. His name was Brendan and he did illustration for the store's fashion ads. He was just always around, and we dated off and on."

"And he did you wrong?" Peter was half-joking, he hoped, one eyebrow raised.

Sister shook her head. "Not the old Victorian cliché," she said. "The fact is, he went into the priesthood. Just like that." She pushed the heavy coffee cup aside. "It was funny that all the time we went together he scarcely ever touched me. He was a talker, amazingly serious for a young man, and I'd begun to think he didn't like me. God knows I certainly liked him. But when he went off to the Church—one day he was here, the next he wasn't—then I realized it was something abstract that drew him to me, maybe something downright *holy*, and the first thing you knew, *I* was the one ready to give my life to the Church. Brendan led the way to it; he'd held the lamp to light my path."

* * *

IT SEEMS TO PETER that the path was never entirely toward the holy, for what emerges from the verses Sister Mary Martha shows him is as much of the flesh as of the spirit. There is in one poem "leaned / against your windowsill / a steep ladder of moonlight / my chaste thoughts climb / to the bed where you naked sleep." In another the poet recalls "my knee touching / yours as we bow beneath / a painted crucifix. / I wonder which is blood / and which mere color. / Genuflection, crucifixion, / the two words whirl themselves / into a third whose syllables / body may not pronounce."

Peter is not sure how to respond to such images. He tries to limit himself to matters of diction, of syntax, avoiding discussions concerning the nature of sexuality repressed or of love's safer alternatives. He says things like "can thoughts be 'chaste' if they are about a naked person?" or "Do you really mean 'may not pronounce' or should you say '*will* not pronounce'?"

What perplexes is that the poems arouse in him emotions he is not supposed to feel. One is not to be attracted to a nun; she is Christ's woman. Yet when he is home at the end of the day, the light fading in his study, the smell of supper filling the small house he shares with his wife, the lines from Sister Mary Martha's poems swim across the currents of his thinking. He sees Sister's face, the pale, earnest features framed by her habit, and though the mouth is solemn, the eyes are mischievous and hold promises better unspoken.

One day she shows him a photograph of herself, taken before she entered the convent. It is at the end of one of their poetry conferences and, as it happens, they have spent much of the hour talking not about Sister's poems, but about those of one of her former pupils, a girl named Connie Lamontagne.

"I knew you'd be good for her," Sister Mary Martha tells him.

"She raves about you, that you know what she means to say even better than she does herself."

"She takes suggestions well," Peter says.

"And you excite her." Sister opens her notebook and turns its pages. "She reminds me of myself when it finally dawned on me what Brendan meant in my life. Here."

She offers him a snapshot: the secular Mary Martha, in a tweed coat and wool scarf, hatless, her hair loose around her smiling face. He guesses she was in her early twenties.

"Brendan took it. Can you see what he meant to me?"

"Yes," Peter says. "It shows in your eyes, your mouth."

Sister takes back the photograph. "That's how Connie looks," she says, "when she talks to me about you."

*　*　*

CONSTANCE THERESA LAMONTAGNE is the latest of Sister Mary Martha's ninth-grade protégées, passed on to Peter with Sister's praise and recommendation: *Connie is a serious young woman with an interest in the sciences, but don't be put off by that. She's a fine writer with a head full of ideas I know you can help her give shape to.*

In her junior year, Connie is a slender sixteen-year-old, with honey-blond hair and pale, almost translucent skin. The hair is straight and long, a breathtaking fall that cascades over her shoulders to the middle of her back in a way that reminds him of the pictures in mythology books of the sirens wooing Odysseus. Her eyes are a pale, mystical blue; Peter has sometimes wondered if she wears contact lenses tinted to reinforce the blueness of her gaze, but he believes not. Nature, or the God he doubts, has created those miraculous irises.

And the brain, the mind, the quickness of her thought in the classroom she shares with him—it is an intelligence that shames all the rest. He sees her in the school lunchroom, natural, joking with boys who are straining to be individual—blackened lower lids, blue hair, studs in their noses, earrings, gold chains with innumerable keys suspended down their thighs. Connie dresses in jeans and sweatshirts, wears white tennies, seems not to own a makeup kit. Her skin is unflawed; her hair, bound into a ponytail, is clean and silken and (he imagines) sweet-smelling, perhaps like a pine forest or a seaside place at high tide. Her only jewelry is a heavy, silver-colored bracelet that rides over the delicate bone of her left wrist. Whose gift? he wonders, and feels an unjustifiable thrill of jealousy. She is one of those achingly pretty girls who is continually shadowed—or stalked—by boys, but Peter cannot imagine that any one of them has found her favor, for there is no boy in the Ducharme school who is not so far beneath Constance Lamontagne as to be an unthinkable partner.

He notices her more times than he can count—in the halls, on the fractured sidewalks in front of the dilapidated school, at the door of the bus that takes her home every afternoon. Each time he sees her he is moved as if for the first time, caught by some aspect of her that he had not yet marked: the way she raises her hand to push back a lock of hair that has fallen to shadow her brow, the melody of her voice as she calls out to a friend, the lift and tilt of her chin as she looks up at the wall-clock in his first-hour class. Is she bored? he wonders. Does she wish he would stop his talk, let her get on with her magical life?

Yet she is attentive to him in ways his other students are not. She stops by his office nearly every afternoon—to talk poetry, to offer him a Coke, to complain about some other Ducharme teacher. If he happens not to be available, she leaves little notes, sometimes only a picture of herself—a smiley face with three squiggly lines on left and right for hair—or a draft of her latest poem. Sister Mary Martha may be right: that he "excites" the Lamontagne girl, that he does know what she means to say, but it is not intuition—merely age and experience and all Peter's classroom years in the midst of adolescent turbulence.

And then again there is the Woman thing: rows and ranks of teen-aged girls on the cusp of maturity, testing their first male teacher against boyfriends, fathers, imagined husbands. How can Peter not feel the pressure of those comparisons, the energies focused on him, the daily provocations of blossoming sexuality? His tiny office seems to him to have become a secular confessional where solemn-faced woman-children tell him in low voices their stories: of menstrua-tion—how their timid mothers lied about its meaning and import, how the odor of their own blood offends them; of learning to mas-turbate—how shame contends with pleasure, how it is a necessary virtue for good Catholic girls because it makes abstinence bearable; how they keep count of their orgasms. *What does this have to do with your poetry?* he wants to ask them, but if he asks he gives the lie to his insistence, his genuine belief, that the best writing proceeds from absolute honesty, perfect truth.

"Those are things women don't even tell other women," his wife says. "How do you get them to do it?"

"Do what?"

"Talk about such intimate matters. What do you ask them, I won-der."

"I don't ask them anything. They talk; I listen."

"But you must say something. My God, I'd never have talked to a teacher of mine, especially a male teacher, about sex."

Peter isn't entirely certain about the grounds from which Shelley is launching this apparent attack on him. Is she envious? It makes no sense for her to be threatened by teenagers. Does she imagine there is something between himself and his students—that he would be stupid enough to risk his marriage, his job, and possibly his liberty by involving himself with a child? *Jailbait*—isn't that the word people used to apply to the female underaged?

"I can't explain it," he says. "I guess they trust me."

"It never happens with boys," she says. "Your male students don't seem to be so goddamned trusting."

"Some of them are. But they aren't as interesting—aren't as imaginative, I mean—as the girls, and I don't tell you about them."

"Hah," Shelley says, a response that makes him feel angry and guilty and superior, all in a single ineffable instant.

He wants to go on to say something pompous about the efficacy of *only listening*, that among other things it's crucial to the workings of Mother Church, that the justification for prayer is entirely dependent on the idea of Someone *only listening*. Father Devon, from his place on the other side of the confessional partition, would surely validate Peter's innocence.

"I don't encourage them," Peter says.

But it occurs to him, just for a moment, that perhaps he is protesting too much—that if he were in fact in the confessional with Father Devon, he might have to admit that his students' intimate revelations please him, because they indeed show trust—he is a "safe" confidant—even when they sometimes embarrass him and perplex his wife.

*   *   *

THIS IS WHY WHENEVER he encourages Sister Mary Martha to reminisce about the convent, he knows—everyone knows—she is not going to ensnare him in some sort of profane carnal web. He is an innocent; he has no designs on her, nor she on him. She is simply open and outgoing. At most, she might be nudging him to recapture his own abandoned faith when she talks about the convent's liturgical routine. It's true that Peter is endlessly curious about what she gave up after her time in the workaday world, and did she regret—

what was his name?—did she regret Brendan and what might have been if he had not chosen the priesthood as his vocation? But Peter never presses, never pries.

Sister has a wealth of anecdotes—activities and occasions that defined the convent for her, shaped her into the teacher she became in the narrow corridors of Ducharme. If the stories are rich in detail, their imagery vivid, sensual—well, he thinks, where is the harm if only his attention is seduced?

She tells him, for example, how only after she had lived in the convent for a year was she permitted to work in the kitchen, and how of all the plain foods she learned to prepare, bread was her favorite. She devised her own secret recipe, created over months of trial that earned her sometimes praise and sometimes penalty, but when at last she was satisfied, it was a recipe others envied but might not aspire to. Nearly every Sunday she was in the kitchen, mixing, stirring, beating—hour upon hour of labor given for the finest possible texture—kneading and letting rise and kneading again and again. She could feel in her arms, her hands, in her fingers, in her shoulders and back, what strength she had, what love impelled her. In summer the perspiration dripped from her face and flowed down her arms as if to leaven the bread; in winter she held the rising dough in its stoneware bowl against her breast, embracing it to protect the yeast from the cold drafts knifing into the kitchen through cracked windowpanes.

Next, she taught herself to slice the bread so exquisitely thin "you might have read a text through it," so thin (she says) one could have imagined repairing the cracked kitchen glass by substituting rose windows whose petals were bread slices, whose leading was crust; so thin that when she arranged two slices side by side on a white plate she told herself she had made a butterfly against the full moon. *Even her memories are poems*, Peter thinks.

He finds Sister Mary Martha's convent stories provocative, her exaggerations charming, but he wonders what he is to make of them, why she shares with him such personal, such *specific* revelations. Ordinarily the two of them don't discuss religion: the Church and what Peter considers its elitism, the disjunction between Catholic policy and real-world practice, the right or wrong of contraception and abortion, and whether faith is a private or a public matter. The stories lead him more and more to questions he prefers to think of as sophomoric—not merely why he has turned away from the Church, but how he feels toward God and His Son and His Son's Mother, how does belief influence his actions in everyday life, what are his views on sin and redemption.

He has not foreseen this; perhaps it genuinely *is* Sister's plan, conscious or not, to coax him once more into the Catholic fold or, at the least, to sensitize him to the importance of his immortal soul. Or it is not Mary Martha's plan, but Father Devon's, passed down from the diocese in the interest of cleansing the Ducharme faculty by reconverting the lapsed.

*　*　*

MOST FRIDAYS, after classes are done for the week, Peter takes charge of detention in the school's modest library, a room containing two long maple conference tables and a dozen seven-foot bookshelves ranked along three walls; the room is windowless, the front wall all blackboard and chalk rail. Detention is punishment for the Ducharme students' various transgressions: contraband food or candy, unruliness during lessons, the vanity of swearing, sarcasm directed at a nun or brother. Detention, an extra hour deprived of weekend light and air, has long since replaced the strap, or the sharp rap of ruler across knuckles Peter recalls from his own early schooling; it is the first line of administrative punishment in a list that moves onward to suspension and, further still, expulsion.

Though detention is perhaps unpleasant for the students, it is almost a pleasure for Peter. Shelley is at the bookstore late on Fridays, so there is no urgency for him to be at home; even when detention is done, he often spends the afternoon and early evening in his office, reading or grading papers. When he does go home, it's to begin the Friday ritual: he puts two stemmed glasses into the freezer compartment, then he mixes manhattans for two, dumps out the ice, and stores the shaker in the freezer compartment against his wife's arrival around seven. Usually they eat at one of Scoggin's three restaurants, none of which has a liquor license; some Fridays, after they have finished their manhattans, they don't go out at all.

Today when detention is over Connie Lamontagne is waiting outside his office door. She wears jeans and a white blouse, tennis shoes and a pale blue sweater. She is sitting on the hall floor, lotuslike, a notebook cradled by her knees, a pencil rested pensively on her lower lip.

"I peeked in at your detention," she says. She gets to her feet as Peter unlocks his office. "I guess half those kids must have been sent there for dressing badly."

"Or for bad dye jobs," he says. He enjoys the sense of sharing conspiracies with her, of being *with* her, allied. It is, he imagines, a way of pretending he is young, and he hopes she doesn't perceive him as pathetic.

He stands aside to let her precede him into the room. The trailing scent of her is like a tangible force that draws him in her wake.

"I sort of miss the middle-school days," Connie says. She sits in the chair that faces his and stacks her textbooks and notebook on the corner of his desk. "You know? When we all had to wear the same clothes?"

Peter sits. "Didn't the uniform stifle the imagination a bit?"

"I don't think so. Imagination is what you do. Not what you wear."

"That's a point," Peter says.

"And I think sometimes if you *look* like everybody else, that makes you free to be really different, deep-down."

Peter makes a tent of his fingers, letting the peak of the tent balance Connie's serious face. Depending on how he moves his head, the joined fingers point to the girl's mouth, one eye, the other eye. . . . He hopes she doesn't think he is staring at her, that she realizes he is being thoughtful, trying to look wise. He is about to comment on this matter of *appearance*—its relationship to hidden individuality—but Connie is frowning and saying something about auras.

"You have a peculiar aura today," she says. "I think you must really hate detention."

"I have an aura?" he says.

"Everybody has auras."

"And you can see mine?"

She runs open fingers through her hair to push it back from her face. "I can see everybody's." She tosses her head and the hair falls again across one cheek. "Don't ask how it happens. I've just always had the ability. Yours is usually white; today it's a sort of pukey yellow."

"I assume the colors mean something," Peter says. He thinks it's what helps make him a successful teacher: this willingness to go along with the most ridiculous statements his students can come up with.

"They do—but the colors mean different things with different people. With you, white is a sort of neutral. Like 'I'm O.K., the world's O.K.' No stress, no bad stuff. But today—" Connie leans forward, elbows on her thighs, hands palm upward as if she is offering him an insight that's palpable, that has veritable shape and weight. "I think detention bums you out."

"Actually, I rather enjoy it," he says. "It's quiet in the library. I can read, or catch up with paper-grading."

"But that's on the surface," she says. "Your aura comes from *within*."

"You mean I think I enjoy detention, but deep-down—your phrase—I hate it, and I don't *know* I hate it."

"Exactly." She sits back in the chair. "Michael's aura is a very pale shade of blue. It's a little like the color of the blue chalk Sister Mary Martha used to use to underline words on the blackboard."

She looks at him, looks through him—or is she noticing how his own aura has suddenly changed at the mention of an unfamiliar name? From pukey yellow to pukey green, for burgeoning jealousy. He clears his throat and swings his knees toward the desk as if he is preparing to commence some necessary work.

"Did I mention I have a boyfriend named Michael?" she says.

"I don't believe you did."

"He's a senior. He's already been accepted at Notre Dame."

"That's impressive," Peter says.

* * *

HE CAN'T SAY HOW HIS ATTRACTION to Connie Lamontagne is altered by the revelation that she has, as his wife might put it, *a beau*. Now when she shows him her poetry, he finds himself searching it for clues to Michael, looking for references to an *other*, reading into the poems their connection with the author's real world. He lectures himself on the subject of the autobiographical fallacy, and tells himself, sternly, that it is foolish of him to spend his time ferreting out the indiscretions of a student. On the other hand, he reminds himself, this is the way he is—it's nothing personal: Constance or Mary Martha or Jane Doe are all the same to him. It is simply part and parcel of his abstract appreciation for Woman. Perhaps it is his mother's fault that women seem to him closer to *secrets*—Peter can't define the word—men may not be privy to.

One day he sees Connie talking with someone he imagines is her friend Michael: a tall, long-haired boy in the kind of heavy coat-sweater athletes wear. Notre Dame probably wants him for basketball, Peter thinks, all other things being equal. Connie looks serious, the boy is listening and nodding, shifting his books from one hand to the other.

Later the same day she comes by the office to show him a new poem—it is about how snow takes color from the clothing of children who play in it. Before he finishes reading it, she says:

"Did you know Sister M.M. before she was a nun?"

"M.M.?"

"Well I didn't mean Marilyn Monroe," she says.

"No," he answers. "I didn't meet her until Ducharme."

"I asked because the two of you seem quite close."

Peter smiles. "We have literature in common," he says.

When they have talked about her poem, and she has scrawled his suggestions—his questions—in the margins of the page, she says, "I didn't mean to be disrespectful."

"You weren't," he says. "As it happens, Sister and I both started here in the same year."

"I knew it had to be something special," Connie says.

"It is."

Connie folds her poem lengthwise and slides the page inside one of her textbooks. Peter moves his feet, ready to stand, but she makes no move to leave. Instead, she leans back in the chair and lets her shoulders slump.

"I've done a really stupid thing," she says.

* * *

ON THE NEXT WEDNESDAY, a cold and rainy one, he is late getting home—a detour to the post office for stamps, a stop at a drugstore where blank videotape is on sale—and when he is hanging his raincoat in the front hall closet he hears voices from the kitchen. Both voices are familiar: his wife's, of course—and Connie Lamontagne's. He thinks he might interrupt by walking into the kitchen, but decides instead to go to his study, where he sits pretending to work until he hears the voices move to the downstairs hall and the front door open and close. He stands at the head of the stairs and sees Shelley just turning away from the door.

"Wasn't that the Lamontagne girl?" he says. It's awkward phrasing; he never thinks of her that way.

"Yes."

"Had you met her before today?"

"She's come by the bookstore a couple of times," Shelley says. "Today she said she wanted to talk privately, so I asked Terri to take over and brought the girl here for hot chocolate."

"What's it all about?" Peter says.

"You don't know?" Shelley says. "You with your talent for drawing out the most personal revelations from your female students?"

"Spare me the sarcasm."

"She's pregnant," Shelley says. "That's all. She missed her period, and then she bought one of those do-it-yourself pregnancy test kits that came out positive."

"Do-it-yourself," he echoes. "That means she might be wrong."

"She might. And she might not. She's missed a second period."

Of course Peter already knows—has heard the whole story from Connie's own lips as she sat that afternoon in his office. He knows who the father is—Michael—and even where it happened: in her parents' bed while the parents were visiting Grandmother Lamontagne in a Portland hospital. If he didn't share the knowledge with Shelley, certainly it was only to avoid yet another critique of his intimate dealings with students.

"So, what is she going to do?"

"I told her I'd take her to the women's clinic. We'll drive down to Boston Saturday morning. Unless something goes wrong, I'll have her home in time for supper."

Peter shivers. He thinks about abortion—and about the efficiency of a procedure that obliterates mortality in time for supper. He is neither "pro-abortion" nor "pro-life," nor can he understand except in the most imagined and distant way the arguments that pivot on the integrity of women's bodies. In the abstract, he despises the fanaticism abortion provokes, and he is angered by the suggestion that if one isn't *for* something, then one must be *against* it—and vice versa. At this moment, in the particular, all he knows is that he wants Connie Lamontagne's life not to be screwed up by one mistake, but something—perhaps a weak echo of the lost faith he argues with Sister—bothers him about his wife's decisiveness.

"Is Connie O.K. with that?" he says. "Does she agree that abortion is the way to go?"

Shelley frowns. "You think she should have the baby? You want your favorite bright student to be a mother at the age of sixteen? Never mind that her father would probably throw her out in the cold."

"I didn't say I wanted her to have it. I asked does she think getting rid of it is the right thing to do."

"Some things you can't let a teenager decide," his wife says. "This is one of them."

"I suppose."

"Think about your own daughter," she says.

And he remembers how he fretted when Jackie, in high school, overstayed her curfew, how he mistrusted her boyfriends—especially the boys with cars—and how many times he had rehearsed in his own mind the possibility of his daughter being pregnant: how would he respond, what would he do?

"Did she tell you who's responsible?"

"One of your good Catholic boys. I was appropriately horrified. She said she asked him if he was taking precautions, but he said no, he wasn't."

"That should have been the end of it," Peter says.

"But don't forget: this was in the heat of the moment." Peter recalls such heat. "What's worse is that apparently she did say to him, 'What if I get pregnant?' And what he said was, 'Then it's God's will.' Can you believe?"

"I can imagine it being said," he tells his wife, "but I can't imagine a woman being persuaded by it."

"Oh, well," his wife says, "'*persuaded.*' That's something else again."

*   *   *

SATURDAY, ALL DAY LONG, Peter is restless, acting in much the way animals behave under sudden changes in the barometer. He wonders what is happening in the weather of his thoughts as he goes from his study, where student writing awaits his red pencil, to the living room, where he turns on the television but doesn't stay to watch anything. Suspended between dangling modifiers and college football, he can opt for neither.

He wonders if he should have talked with Sister about the implications, spiritual and secular, of abortion. Here was a real-world matter appropriate to their occasional discussions of Catholic policy and protocol. Here was an opportunity to forswear abstraction, to talk about two actual students known to them both. Now that the deed is done, who is sinner, who sinned against?

At a little after six-thirty he hears Shelley's car in the driveway—the engine stopped, a door slamming closed. Peter turns off the television, settles himself in his armchair and adopts an attitude of alert concern. Shelley comes in alone, bringing the cold outside air with her. She takes off her orange quilted jacket and sits with it in her lap on the sofa opposite Peter.

"How did it go?" he asks.

"Let me unwind for a minute," she says. "Maybe you could mix a manhattan."

"You bet." He badly wants to ask about the clinic, the drive, the medical procedure, though he is not exactly sure how to phrase the questions. He mixes the drinks, pours them—Shelley's on the rocks, his own in a stemmed glass—and delivers hers to her. She holds the jacket up to him and he takes it and hangs it in the front hall closet.

When he comes back into the living room Shelley is cradling the glass but not drinking. She looks tired, frazzled, the way she is sometimes when she works late at the bookstore and wants to complain to him about encounters with evil customers.

"You all right?" he says.

"I don't want to do that again. Not ever."

"I should have been the one to do it," he says.

"Oh, Peter, that's insane. You're the last person on earth." Now she drinks.

Of course she is right. He has imagined himself in Boston, sitting in the old Subaru at the edge of the clinic parking lot, watching Connie Lamontagne disappear behind the clinic doors—going in alone because of course her teacher dares not be mistaken for the father. The scene is vivid in his mind's eye: only two or three other cars in the lot, the pavement gray and rain-washed, the clinic housed in a low, windowless building—the *abattoir*—that swallows up the forlorn child he has delivered a hundred awkward miles. No, he could never have managed it; he truly *is* the last person on earth.

"Did you leave Connie in Boston?" It seems to him possible that she would need to recuperate, that the complex and delicate mechanisms of Woman would require time and quiet to recover.

"No, no. I drove her home. She seemed fine."

"What did you tell the parents?"

"Shopping trip," Shelley says. "I bought her a cashmere sweater."

"Was it difficult—the abortion thing?"

"It's ridiculously simple," Shelley says. "It makes you wonder."

*   *   *

WHEN SHELLEY IS IN THE BIG BED beside him, propped against the pillows with her hair loose over her shoulders, she looks like the woman Peter knew nearly thirty years ago. No wonder he loves her; no wonder he wanted children with her. There is a photograph she sent him then—somewhere he still has it, squirreled away in the depths of a desk drawer—taken at the shore. She is lying on the beach at Ogunquit, left cheek resting against her right hand, palm flat against the smooth sand, her face sultry and lovely as a mermaid's: this is what Peter sees, watching her now in the room's dim lamplight. He realizes this is one more of those intimations of mortality that touch us as we age: how gravity favors us when our faces are turned upward; how it punishes us when we look down. It transcends religion, this awareness—or, he is beginning to think, it cries out for it.

They are both reading—or, rather, Peter has been pretending to read. The truth is that he is increasingly preoccupied with his work at school, and how in the few weeks since Connie's confession the whole atmosphere of his vocation has changed. It is as if his renunciation of faith so many years back has finally had a consequence—a delayed revelation of what it means to reject even a disinterested God. Now he feels exiled, alone in a Ducharme community that had formerly nurtured him, fulfilled him, even kept him attached to Woman, as colleague, as pupil.

"I wonder if we did the right thing after all," he says.

His wife lowers her magazine. "About what?"

"You know. Taking Connie to Boston," as if Boston—like New York City in his youth—were the transgression, and the murder of a fetus merely incidental.

"I'll say it again," Shelley tells him. "She was too young to make the decision. She'll thank us when she's grown up."

She raises the magazine, and Peter marvels at the difference between his wife and his colleague: how the one is so confidently dismissive of the case, while for the other there can be neither forgetting nor forgiving what Connie must have told her. Sister Mary Martha barely acknowledges him in the school corridors; she no longer speaks to him. He cannot even ask if Father Devon has heard the girl's confession—if in spite of her actions she has been reconciled with the Church.

All Sister's attentions are turned, apparently, toward Constance Lamontagne. The two appear inseparable; he scarcely ever sees one without the other. As for Connie, she has become only a vague recollection of closer times. Lately there have been no more notes, no more self-caricature with the squiggly hair, no more after-school interpretation of his aura. Peter has never known such loneliness.

Now, as he is about to put his book aside and turn out the light, he hears a siren outside. Fire truck, ambulance, Peter isn't sure which, but on this crisp winter night just before Christmas, no wind, living as he does on the edge of town away from traffic, the siren sound is as clear as breaking crystal. *Si-reen*, say the town's French-Canadian children.

He gets out of bed to look out the window. His wife closes her magazine.

"What's that racket?" she says. "What's going on?"

"Fire," he says. "Must be big."

Because now he hears a newer, closer siren. It dopplers past the house, and this means the fire equipment from Springvale, two miles north of Scoggin, has been called in. Standing at the bedroom window that faces toward the town center, Peter sees framed in a half-oval of frost at the bottom of the window pane a sky dancing with yellow-orange auras, like Northern Lights without the blue-green dazzle of arctic ice.

"I think it's the school," he tells her.

Shelley comes to the window and stands beside him. "My God," she says. Her perfume—something lilac, lingering from her daytime self—is nearly aphrodisiac. He has to step away from the window, from his wife.

"I'm going to drive over. See what's going on."

He gets dressed, sweeps his keys off the dresser. As he leaves the room, his wife goes back to bed and picks up the novel he has been reading.

"Don't lose my place," he says.

* * *

HE PARKS THE SUBARU down the hill on Nason Street and trots toward the school. Even though the Scoggin fire station is only three short blocks away, he can see that the matter is hopeless. Flames are already leaping above the roofline, and heat has broken out the glass of all—or nearly all—the windows facing the street. There are fire trucks, police cars, precautionary ambulances ringing the area. Peter can see a pumper training water on the roof of the Knights of Columbus home behind the school, where the teaching brothers have upstairs apartments. Despite the late hour, a crowd has gathered, standing among the vehicles, fascinated by the fire. "It had to be the wiring," somebody says. And another voice echoes: "They say it was wiring in the attic." The attic, Peter knows, is where the archives are kept—the records of Maurice Ducharme, his faith, his celebrity, his school.

When the roof falls in there is an enormous increase in light and heat, a shower of great orange sparks, a flaring-up of yellow flame half again the height of the building. Everyone recoils from the event, falling back two or three steps, sending up a collective gasp of shock and fright. The heat is terrific, forcing the onlookers to retreat and turn their faces away. The light is for an instant physical; people in the crowd put their hands up to shield themselves. Peter can make out individual wooden beams, black and rimmed with small petals of flame, already burned out and useless for support. They fall in pairs and threes from the top of the school, down through the third, the second, the first floors, down into the below-ground church, where prayers have always begun every school day. He imagines his office falling, there, at that front corner of the school: the cluttered desk and the file cabinets, the chair where Connie sat weeping for being "stupid," the steel bookcase with its anthologies and grammar texts and the Bible his mother gave him for his First Communion— the only religious relic he still kept.

He looks away from the school. His face turns cold, and in that sharpened instant he discovers Connie Lamontagne and Sister Mary Martha standing side by side. He wonders how long they've been here, only a few feet behind him, not joining him. Connie's eyes are uplifted and bright with reflected fire, her young skin ruddy from flame, damp with perspiration; her mouth is half opened as if from surprise or delight—or as if she sees something more than fire, something that might make sense to Sister Mary Martha but seems now forever denied to him. The two women might be siblings, wrapped in each other's arms, their eyes uplifted, their faces *suffused*—there is no better word—with the radiance of the flames. Peter tries to work his way to them through the crowd, but by the time he reaches the place where he saw them they are gone.

Driving home, he wonders how he will ever recover his center— that necessary still point around which his life has for so long traced its circles—now that the Ducharme community is homeless. He will see even less of Sister. He will rarely see Connie Lamontagne except in some unlikely classroom temporary and secular—the Town Hall auditorium, the Scoggin Trust Community Room, the basement of the Masonic Temple—each space echoing with the clatter and scrape of metal folding chairs. And what is it Peter imagines he needs? Pushing through the gawkers toward his lost women, perhaps he had only wanted to ask: *But who will read your poems? And who will hear your secrets?*

Mind's Eye

The pain in his eyes was extraordinary, and because he couldn't see, there was no distraction from it. He couldn't read a magazine or look around at the pictures on the walls of the waiting room. He couldn't name the plants whose potted earth was a small but acrid odor in his nostrils. He couldn't determine if the receptionist was the same one who had worked here the last time he had an eye exam. He could only sit, the faint aura of canned music washing over him, his daughter's hand holding his, as if without her touch he might lose his nerve and run.

"How're you doing?" she said.

"Hurting," he said. "You can't believe."

"He'll give you something for the pain. You'll be fine."

She patted his hand; the gesture made him feel like an old man, but he didn't tell her that. He was glad for her help—coming when he called, driving him here—and it would have been ungrateful of him to be critical.

"I can use it," he said.

Now a blur of white shimmered before him.

"Mr. Reece? We're ready for you now."

He stood, his hand still in his daughter's. "Is it all right if Jenny stays with me?"

"Certainly."

The doctor's assistant preceded him. He let Jenny be his guide, steer him around whatever furniture might have got in his way.

"I hope you don't mind being needed," he said.

*　*　*

HE SAT IN A NARROW CHAIR that smelled of vinyl, waiting for Doctor Gavin to attend to him. Arthur Gavin was affable, conservative, an acquaintance and fellow country club member for twenty years, but never what you could call a close friend. He sat at a desk nearby, a shadow against a lamp, turning pages of some sort.

"Three years since your last exam, Hal," Gavin said. "Almost four. Any problems? I mean until today."

"None," Reece said. "I've torn a couple of lenses, but I'm told that's par for the course."

He remembered his last visit, the end of it when the doctor switched on the overhead lights—how the examining room reappeared, beginning to seem familiar: the posters of cross-sectioned eyeballs, the cabinet slotted to hold steel-rimmed lenses, the caddy bearing its variety of eye drop vials. Dominating everything was wallpaper that depicted a nature scene—background mountains, foreground a rushing of blue and white rapids. Today all such detail was lost in a fog, mostly blue.

"I'm really hurting," Reece said.

"Mmm," Gavin said. "I want you to lean forward, rest your chin here. Can you see this contraption?"

"Sort of."

"Here," Gavin said. "A little closer—push with your forehead. That's it."

Reece felt the coolness of the strap on his brow. He pressed against it. A sudden vivid light burst into his eyes.

"Tell me again what happened," Gavin said.

"It must have been the saline solution," Reece said. "A different brand from the kind I normally use. As soon as I got the contacts in, I knew something was wrong. My eyes stung like fury."

"Mmm."

The light turned to blue. It played in a slow arc across Reece's field of vision, left eye, then right, and back again.

"I took the lenses out, rinsed them under the tap. Then I scrounged around and located what was left of the old saline stuff. I used that to put the contacts back in."

"Soft contacts, you said?"

"We went to those when I was in here before. Three years ago."

"Mmm. I remember."

"I went on to school," Reece said. "I was halfway through my ten o'clock when things began to blur. By the end of the hour I was blind. And scared. I had a student lead me back to my office."

Gavin was looking at the right eye. "You've got damage to both corneas," he said. "Chemical burns—"

"Jesus," Reece said.

"The left is just a bit worse than the right, but I think you'll be O.K. with a little t.l.c."

"That's my job," Jenny said. She had been sitting in the corner of the room nearest the door, quiet, almost invisible in shadow. Gavin half-turned in his chair, as if he were noticing her for the first time.

"This can't be Jennifer, can it?"

"It is," she said.

Gavin returned his attention to Reece. "Harold? Is it possible that *you* fathered this lovely woman?"

"She takes after her mother," Reece said.

"Ah, that explains it." Gavin went to his desk and came back to stand over Reece. "I'm going to put some drops in," he said. "These'll numb you a little; ought to reduce the immediate pain somewhat."

The drops were cold; he tensed, and tried to close each eye as he sensed the nearness of the dropper, but Gavin held the lids open. The pain throbbed and diminished in a rhythm tuned to his heart. He relaxed.

"And I'm going to put in a therapeutic lens—kind of a miniature contact lens—to protect the corneas while they heal. Just leave them in until I see you again."

"How long?"

"Hard to say." Gavin placed the contacts, left then right. He scanned the sharp blue light across Reece's eyes. "If you have any problem, call right away. Otherwise, come in day after tomorrow. Phyllis will set up a time for you."

"All right."

Gavin sat at the desk and scrawled a prescription. "This is for Tylenol with codeine. I wouldn't take it unless the pain keeps you awake. And if you take it you shouldn't drink; it might make you sick." He handed the slip of paper to Jenny. "Make him behave himself," he said.

"It's too late for that," she said.

* * *

"I HATE BANTER," Jenny said. She gave the car too much gas, and the rear tires shrieked. The car jolted onto the highway, turning toward the lowering sun.

"What provokes that?"

"You know: 'Is it possible you fathered this lovely woman?' Stuff like that."

"He was just noticing how grown-up you are." Reece put up one hand against the glare and lowered the visor with the other. "He hasn't seen you since long before the divorce."

"He could have spoken to *me*," she said, "instead of bantering with you."

"Art Gavin and I go way back," Reece said. "He's a Stone-Age Republican. He never passes up a chance to needle me."

"It must be some perverse male-bonding thing," Jenny said. "Do you want me to take you back to campus?"

"I'd better go home. The car's safe in the university garage. Anyway, I'd be a menace on the highway."

"What will you do about your three o'clock?"

"I'll call the department secretary. She'll send someone over to dismiss them."

"Lucky class," Jenny said. "The gift of a free hour."

"I'd rather imagine them deeply disappointed."

She looked at him, then looked back at the highway. He could make out the pale bloom of her face, and then it vanished, like a dim light going out.

At the pharmacy, Jenny trotted in to fill his prescription while Reece waited. His isolation felt complete; the one or two people who passed the window of the car were as blind to him as he was to them. Then they were at the house, the windows of its twin gables a dazzle in the afternoon sunlight. Jenny stopped in front of the garage on his side of the duplex, shifted into park.

"I'm grateful for the taxi service," Reece said. "I know you have a life of your own."

"Don't mention it. Think of it as me paying you back for all the times you chauffeured me when I was a little kid."

"Your mother did most of that."

"But you were the one who always drove me to piano lessons."

"You remember that, do you?" In the instant, in his mind's eye, he was behind the wheel of the old Rambler station wagon, turning onto Ash Street, stopping at Lisa's white ranch house.

"Every Tuesday at four," Jenny said. "What was that woman's name?"

"Howard," Reece said. *Memorable.* "Lisa Howard."

"Of course you'd remember *that*," she said.

"But I'd forgot all those tedious lessons of yours."

"Me too. The only pieces I can play now are 'I Love Coffee, I Love Tea' and 'Für Elise.'"

"You can't blame me," he said. "You ought at least to know 'Chopsticks.'"

He folded back the sun visor and cracked open the car door.

"I talked to Ma yesterday," Jennifer said. *Out of the blue.* "She wondered if you remembered that last Tuesday would have been your twenty-fifth anniversary."

"It crossed my mind."

"But you didn't do anything about it?"

"That was a long time ago," he said. "Jesus H. Your mother and I have been divorced nearly ten years."

"I told her about your eye problem. She said at least you wouldn't be looking at other women for a while."

"Sweet," he said, "and very funny." He pushed the door all the way open and slid out.

"Wait a sec." She caught his hand, holding him half in and half out of the car. Her voice softened. "Are you O.K. alone? Should I stay?"

"I'm fine," he said. "Really."

"I don't want you falling downstairs."

"I think I can see enough to survive," he said.

"At least let me walk you to your door."

*   *   *

AFTER HIS SUPPER—A FROZEN PIZZA, its cooking time guessed at because he couldn't read the back of the package, and a glass of white wine, warm, because he'd forgotten to chill a new bottle—he sat in the leather chair in his empty living room. There wasn't much to do. He couldn't read or grade papers, didn't want to watch a television of blurry shadows. He couldn't even make out the headlines of the newspaper he'd brought in that morning, before he started to put in his contacts.

He closed his useless eyes. *Lisa Howard.* The name was a nudge, a perverse encouragement. He couldn't blame his daughter for bringing it up; she hadn't known until long after the weekly lessons— after the inevitable divorce. Weighing the name now in his painful dark, he thought he could see again the swirls of snow sliding across the hood of the old Rambler, melting and vanishing and revivifying in the tug between the cold wind and the heat radiating from the hood. He saw himself adjusting the heater and defroster levers to keep the windshield from fogging, and out that windshield the outlines of the piano teacher's house with its picture window that overlooked the front yard's winter-smothered yews.

And he could see on one magic occasion the unexpected vision of the piano teacher herself, a pale image in the picture window, waving, beckoning. At first he had thought it was a trick of the storm, a snow figure shaped by wind. Then he realized Lisa Howard was no mirage, but a real person inviting him out of his car. But for what? Something about little Jenny, surely. Was the girl ill? Or, no, had she so distinguished herself in the day's lesson that her father was being called to witness, to join in the praise?

He had shut off the engine and gone to the house, head down against the wind-driven snow, the tiny flakes stinging his face as he picked his way—no haste-making on that slippery driveway—to the front door, which opened to him the moment he arrived at its threshold. The piano teacher held the door while he came into a front hallway that held a hat rack, an umbrella stand, a bronze-framed wall mirror.

"Take off your coat," the teacher said. "We still have a half-hour to go, but it seemed cruel to leave you sitting out there in the storm."

"It's kind of you, Ms. Howard."

"Lisa, please." She took his overcoat and hung it alongside the mirror. "Can I get you something? There's coffee. There's even whiskey, but you mustn't tell the other parents."

"I'll be fine," Reece said.

By this time she had led him into the front room whose windows he had so often watched from his car. At the end of the room was a closed door; he could hear his daughter's clumsy music behind it.

"I have to get back to Jenny," the teacher said. "Why don't you make yourself comfortable. The whiskey is in the kitchen—through there—in the cupboard above the sink. Glasses to the left. Ice—" She stopped. "Well, you know where to find ice."

She left the room. For a few minutes Reece sat on a sofa under the windows. He looked through magazines piled on a coffee table in front of him, listened to Jenny's playing, checked his watch. Finally he went out to the kitchen. He found a bottle of Jack Daniel's, half-filled a tumbler with ice cubes and poured whiskey over them. Then he went back to the front room to drink and wait for the end of the lesson.

That was the beginning of the end of the marriage: a Jack-rocks in the front parlor, sitting under the picture window, watching the wind-driven snow outside while his daughter's music played in muffled fits and starts behind a closed door.

* * *

HE SLEPT BADLY, dozing and starting awake when light from passing cars washed across the bedroom ceiling. The pain persisted, pulsing behind his eyes, and for the first time he wondered if Gavin might be wrong, that the damage wouldn't repair itself, that he would be forever—what was it they called it?—"vision impaired" or, worse, "legally blind." *Nonsense*, he told himself. *Nonsense. I should only have taken the painkillers.*

But the fear stayed with him, until finally he crawled out of bed to escape it. He put on the clothes he had worn the day before— easier than fumbling through his closet and dresser drawers—and came carefully downstairs. The world was still dark, the fan light over the stove a pale porcelain reflection that showed no detail.

He was used to living alone. It was nearly eight years since Lisa had left him to go back to conservatory, and over that time he had perfected the ritual of his mornings. Coffee from the pot that brewed two cups only. Orange juice. A multi-vitamin augmented by a vitamin-E capsule. On the days he taught—usually Tuesdays and Thursdays—he toasted an English muffin, drenched the two halves in butter and ate them with his coffee, sitting in front of *Local on the 8s.*

Today he simplified his routine, omitting the coffee and moving directly to the orange juice, which he managed by resting the spout of the juice carton against the rim of the glass before he poured. He left the orange juice on the counter while he took down the vitamins from their jars in the cupboard, but when he turned to reach for the glass he knocked it over. While he held the glass upright and refilled it, he could hear the spilled juice dripping onto the kitchen floor. If he truly went blind, would every day begin like this one?

After he had swallowed his vitamins and managed to find the weather channel—twenty percent chance of showers, temperature in the low seventies—he phoned Gavin's office. "Arthur said if I had problems, I should come in today," he told Phyllis. "I hope he can work me in."

Reece heard the hollowness of a hand placed over a telephone mouthpiece, muffled words, then Gavin was on the line.

"Hal? What's the difficulty?"

"The pain's been pretty bad," Reece said. "I wasn't able to get much sleep."

"Did you take that high-octane Tylenol I wrote up for you?"

"I'd had a couple of glasses of wine. I didn't want to make myself sick."

There was a pause, and the faint sound of pages turning. "You'll have to come in after regular hours," Gavin said. "I can't manage it any sooner. Say five-thirty—six, to be safe."

"Six is fine," Reece said. "Thanks."

He broke the connection, then dialed Jenny's cell phone. The call went directly to her voice mail.

"I'm afraid I need you today after all," he said. "I had kind of a bad night. Can you take me to see Gavin around a quarter to six today? It's O.K. if you can't. Just call me and I'll get a cab."

* * *

AT TWENTY TO SIX HE HEARD the car in the driveway. He swept his keys off the kitchen counter, stood for a long moment on the back stoop coaxing his house key to find the dead-bolt lock, then followed the iron railing slowly down the steps. It wasn't until he had opened the door to a half-forgotten perfume that he realized it was his ex-wife's car, the blue Civic he had bought her as part of the divorce settlement. Ten years old; she ought to have traded it in long ago.

"Margaret," he said.

How long since he had seen her, talked with her? Early in the divorce the three of them had reunited every June, on Jenny's birthday, and again at Christmas—a neat bisecting of the year—but that ritual was abandoned when Jenny turned eighteen. Jenny's idea, he remembered. *Haven't you had enough pretending?*

His wife turned her face toward him, a pale oval floating in the shadow of the car's interior. "Well? Are you getting in?"

He slid onto the passenger seat and shut the door. Margaret put the car in gear and drove, both hands on the wheel. The car passed through several intersections, no words spoken.

Finally she said, "How are the eyes today? Jenny said you were blind."

"Practically."

"Do you have much pain?"

"Some. It's a little better this afternoon." He ransacked his mind for conversation topics, finding none worthwhile. What had they ever found to talk about? How had they managed thirteen years of marriage? "I suppose it was Jenny's idea," he said, "your picking me up."

"What makes you say that?"

"Yesterday she was hinting for us to get back together," he said. "Brought up our silver anniversary. This must be phase two of the plan."

"Don't flatter yourself. Jenny has an evening class." She pulled into the empty clinic lot, parked close to the entrance and shut down the engine. "Living by yourself must be turning you into a conspiracy freak."

"Sorry," he said, but as he opened the door Margaret put her hand on his sleeve.

"Wait," she said. "I'll come around."

When he got out of the car she was ready to take his arm, closing the door behind him. She steered him up the building's steps by pressure against his elbow. *Was that necessary?* The door ahead was visible, a blurred rectangle darker than its surround, and he thought about shaking off Margaret's guidance, but then he stumbled against a step.

"Whoops," she said. "You really *are* blind."

"I'm fine," Reece said.

"Just don't be a martyr." She opened the door for him. In the waiting room she turned him over to Phyllis, whose white uniform was as dazzling as before.

*　*　*

GAVIN WAS READY FOR HIM. "I watched you pull in," he said. "Was that Margaret driving?" He drew his chair toward Reece and swung the apparatus into place between them. "Are you two getting back together?"

"Jenny had a class," Reece said. "Margaret and I aren't reconciling—if that's what they call it."

"Too bad," Gavin said. He leaned forward. "So then, what's the matter?"

"That throbbing kind of pain," Reece said. "I must have lain awake till three—thinking about the missed classes, errands undone. Silly stuff."

"Nothing to do with a guilty conscience, I hope." Gavin bent forward. "Keep your forehead tight against the strap. You know the drill. Don't raise your chin."

"I was remembering when I was a kid," Reece said. "We lived with my grandmother, who was already well into her seventies. She was forever complaining about her eyesight."

"Mmm," said Gavin. Now he was peering into Reece's left eye, Reece's forehead once more pressed against the cool metal of the headrest.

"She'd say, 'I'm having another one of my blurs.' I was never sure what that meant until the last year or so."

"How's that?" said Gavin. He moved his light to the right eye; its pinpoint made a thin snakelike thread as it crossed Reece's field of vision.

"Because it's started happening to me. The blurs. Every now and then I get this funny sort of shimmer between me and the world. You know how on those cop documentaries they hide somebody's identity by distorting the image? It looks like their faces turn into a bunch of squares, and they flicker as they move?"

"Migraine," Gavin said.

"No. There's no headache."

Dr. Gavin leaned away from him. "Ocular migraine," he said. "There needn't be any headache. Is this a frequent thing?"

"Not really. Now and then. Two or three times a month. I can't predict it."

"Could be stress," Gavin said. "Something as simple as that."

The doctor backed away from the apparatus, his chair wheels a rumbling across the linoleum, and switched on the overhead lights.

"I don't know," Reece said. "I get the feeling that everything about me is deteriorating slowly but surely. You know that chiropractic office Ben Furey has, over near the Sycamore Mall?"

"Know it well," Gavin said.

"The other day—it was long before the evil saline solution—I was driving out Sycamore Avenue when I saw this sign that said 'Fuzzy Chipmunks.' Of course, once I got closer I could see it said 'Furey Chiropractic.'" Reece stood up. "That's what I mean by deterioration. I've lost my distance vision."

"I wouldn't worry," Gavin said. "The important thing here is that you're coming along fine. Just a few more days, a week at the most, your vision should be back to normal. Meanwhile, take that Tylenol."

* * *

AT HOME REECE WALKED from the car with Margaret alongside, though this time she made no move to help him up his steps. He stood at the door for longer than was comfortable, using both hands to work the lock—his left hand locating the keyhole, the right inserting the key.

"I appreciate your patience," he said.

She laughed. "How formal."

"Well I do appreciate it." He pushed open the door and preceded her inside. "You didn't have to do any of this."

"I don't mind."

"I could have got a taxi."

"You don't need to go on about it," she said. "I know you think you walked away for good on the day you called me by that other woman's name in bed. But you didn't walk away. We're both still here."

"You see marriage differently," Reece said.

"And you don't see at all."

"Very funny."

In the living room the curtains were closed, but it didn't matter; if he really did go blind, dark and light would be all the same to him.

"Sit here," Margaret said. She steered him to the leather chair. "Are you hungry? Can I fix you something before I go?"

"It's all right," he said. He leaned his head against the chair back. The pain was faint now, scarcely a bother. "I should probably take a couple of those pills."

"Where are they?"

"On the kitchen counter."

"I'll get you a glass of water."

He heard her in the kitchen—the rattle of glassware, water running and stopping, running and stopping. Now she was beside his chair. He took the water glass with both hands.

"Here," she said. "Two capsules."

He swallowed them and handed back the glass. "Thank you."

"I cleaned up that mess in the kitchen. It looked like orange juice."

"I couldn't see to mop it up," he said.

"What about something to eat?"

"I'll be fine," he said. "Don't worry about me."

"Why don't I make you a fried-egg sandwich. You used to like those. It only takes a couple of minutes."

She was already out of the room. He heard the frying pan, the breaking of an egg, the sizzle. In no time she had thrust a plate into his hands and he was eating the familiar sandwich—the fried egg, a slice of cheddar, a touch of mustard on the rye bread.

"I noticed there's an almost empty bottle of wine in the fridge," Margaret said. "Do you want some?"

"No, thank you."

"Then I'm going to pour myself what's left," she said, "if you don't mind."

"I don't."

She sat across from him beside the bookcase while he finished the sandwich in silence.

Margaret sighed. "You should probably sleep," she said. "I'd better head home and let you recover."

"No need to rush," he said.

She stood and came to him. "If you need anything else, you can call me."

"I'll remember."

"Get some rest. I'll wash up and put the dishes in the drainer."

"Thank you."

She paused in the doorway, a blurred silhouette against the light from the kitchen. "This isn't forgiveness," she said.

The Phoenix Agent

He was tall and good-looking and fiftyish—older than her mother, but not what you would call *old*. He was deeply tanned, with character lines at the corners of his eyes that suggested he either did a lot of squinting into the sun, or laughed a lot, or maybe both. He looked to her like one of those White Hunters you saw in the black-and-white jungle films that turned up on the movie channels—one of those men who was always seducing the wife of the rich guy who was paying for the safari but was wimpy to the core. This man was too cool.

Cinda had never seen him before. She'd been working at the Eco-Mart since the summer before her senior year—now graduation was only three months away—and she was almost sure this was his first appearance in the store. If she'd needed confirmation, she got it almost immediately while she was ringing him up.

"This is quite a market," he said. "A terrific selection of health stuff."

"We think so," she said. She was in the midst of scanning his "stuff"—nut bread, organic peanut butter, broccoli and carrots. "We're not as big as the chains, like Whole Foods, but people like us."

"The personality makes a difference." He was leaning in to read her name tag. "Folks like you, Cinda."

"Thank you." Now she was wary. Was he hitting on her, like some kind of pervo creep, or was he really being nice? She went on scanning his purchases: milk, deli turkey slices, two boxes of loose tea. The jumbo box of detergent he had let stay in the cart, and she reached over the counter to hit the product code with the hand scanner.

"Good shot," the man said.

"Excuse me?" She rang up his total.

"It always impresses me, the way checkout clerks zap the UPC's— like a cowboy shooting from the saddle."

"Your total is eighteen eighty," Cinda said. She began putting the groceries into paper bags.

He held a credit card out to her. "What do you suppose is the range of one of those things?"

She took the card and slid it through the reader. "Range?" she said.

"How far away can you stand and still hit the code?"

She looked at the front of the card—*Edward Hansen*—and the signature on the back, before she handed it back to him. "I've no idea," she said.

* * *

CINDA TOLD HER MOTHER about Edward Hansen over supper that evening.

"He's sort of a hunk," she said, "but weird, you know?"

"It sounds as if he was just being friendly," her mother said. "Making conversation."

"Some conversation: how good a shot am I with the stupid scanner."

"You say you've never seen him before," her mother went on. "If he's new in Orlando he probably doesn't have many friends. You can't blame him for reaching out."

Cinda looked scornful. "Is that what you call it? 'Reaching out'?"

"Don't poke fun," her mother said.

"And anyway, how do you know he's not just a handsome pedophile? And what he's actually reaching out for, you wouldn't care to know."

"*Cinda*," her mother said.

Mother disapproved of worst-case scenarios.

*   *   *

"It's a curious name: Cinda," Edward Hansen said. "I mean it's unusual."

This was the second time she'd checked him out. Whether it was only the second time he'd shopped at EcoMart, she couldn't say, since she worked only Sundays and Wednesdays.

"It's just Linda with a 'C,'" she said. "Your total is twelve twenty-six."

This time he gave her a twenty, one of the newer bills with the giant numbers so nursing-home types could read them. You had to hold up the twenties and look for the little silver thread; if somebody gave you a fifty or a hundred, you had to call for the supervisor.

"I'm sure it's real," Hansen said. "I just got it from your ATM at the back of the store."

"You never know who to trust," Cinda said. "Your change is seven seventy-four." She put the coins in his palm and laid the bills on top of them.

"That's very good," he said.

"Excuse me?"

"Some clerks put the coins on top of the bills—so they can slide off."

"I don't even think about it," she said. "Have a nice day."

He picked up the brown bag. "Have you tested the range of that hand scanner?" He made a pistol of his free hand—forefinger aimed and thumb cocked. "Zap," he said. "I wonder if it could read the code on that *TV Guide* at the next checkout stand."

"I seriously doubt it," she said. The magazine was on a rack that was about five feet away, and the product code was half covered by an astrology paperback.

"Have you tried it?"

"I have better things to do."

She began sliding the next customer's items across the scanner glass. Edward Hansen cradled his bag of groceries and moved away.

"You should give it a shot," he said. "A fair test."

* * *

"What does this Hansen person look like?" her mother wanted to know. "You're certainly paying a lot of attention to him."

"Because he pays attention to me," Cinda said. They were sitting by the pool, side by side on plastic deck chairs. It was Saturday afternoon, early April, hot. "I don't invite it. Honestly."

"Does he remind you of your father?"

"God, Mother. No, he does *not* remind me of Daddy. Besides, I don't remember Daddy all that well." She squeezed sunblock into her hand and smeared the goop on her legs. "He looks kind of like an over-the-hill lifeguard. Tanned, bushy hair that's going gray around his ears, blue eyes—that really pale blue, you know? So pale, he might have come from 'The Village of the Damned.'"

"Is that a book?"

"A horror movie. All the children in the village have eyes with pupils so pale and washed out, you can, like, see right into their heads."

Mother wrinkled her nose. "Not my idea of handsome," she said.

"No, but he *is*. A nice shy smile. A husky voice, like maybe he's a smoker—except he isn't, because I can smell nicotine a mile off."

Her mother smiled and gave a mock sigh. "A shame he's too old for you."

"But not for you," Cinda said. "For you he'd be just right."

"Said the baby bear."

"It's his fussiness that's the only drawback." Cinda stretched and stood up. She pulled the bottom edges of the swimsuit over her buttocks and went into the water. She stood on the floor of the pool, her elbows on the edge, her chin in her hands. "Who notices whether you put the change on top of the dollar bills, or the dollar bills on top of the change? Who the hell cares?"

"Language, Cinda," her mother said.

*   *   *

JUST AT THE END OF HER SHIFT the next day, she saw Edward Hansen go through Veronica Ivey's checkout lane, and she wondered what he was saying to Ronnie—did he have a regular "line" that he practiced on every cashier he met, or what. She ran the total on her register tape and carried the money drawer into the cash-up room behind the deli section.

She finished counting down her day's receipts, then went to the back room to clock out. When she was done with that, and tossed her apron into the laundry hamper, she gathered up her bag and went to wait for Mother. Hansen was sitting at one of the tables at the front of the store, eating a deli sandwich and drinking an organic soda. His bag of groceries sat at his elbow.

"Hello," he said. "The line was shorter at Veronica's register, so I stood you up."

"No problem," Cinda said. "We both work for the same company."

"She puts the coins on top," he said.

"Oh, my God," Cinda said. She hitched the bag higher on her shoulder. "Please don't get her fired."

He smiled. "I bet you're waiting for your mom," he said. "Can I buy you a drink?"

"No, thanks." She sat across the table from him. "But thank you for offering."

"That door behind the deli department," Hansen said. "Is that where the cashiers add up the day's receipts?"

"Yes."

"If the money in your cash drawer doesn't match the total on the register tape, do you girls have to make up the difference?"

"We have to count down until it balances. And it isn't only cash. There's credit card slips, and usually a few checks, and store coupons—a lot of different sub-counts." She frowned at him. "Why? Are you planning to rob the store?"

He looked surprised. "What makes you say that?"

"Your curiosity about how we do things. How we count the receipts. All your questions."

"Would I get away with it?"

She shrugged. "Probably not. Especially if you tried to hold us up with a scanner gun."

He laughed—a kind of bark, short and finished, as if he didn't want to make too much out of laughing. "Right," he said. "Then it's a good thing I'm not a holdup man."

She dragged her bag up to the top of the table, to get the weight of it off her shoulder.

"What *is* your work?" she said. "If robbery's not it."

"I'm almost sorry you asked," he said. "It so happens that I'm between jobs right now, taking a sort of vacation."

"Did you get fired?"

He smiled. "No. I quit."

"That's what everybody says."

"Though in this case it's true," he said. "I had a disagreement with the boss, and I left the company. It was basically a breach of trust."

Cinda looked past him, out the windows to the parking lot. Her mother had left the Volvo wagon in the EcoMart fire lane and was coming into the store.

"Here's my mother," Cinda said. "Illegally parked as usual."

Hansen turned to look as her mother came toward them.

"Mother, this is Mr. Hansen," Cinda said. "The man I've been telling you about."

Hansen stood and bobbed his head. "Edward," he said.

Her mother extended her hand to let Hansen touch it, then withdrew it. "Beth," she said. "My daughter tells me you're a great person for details."

He looked amused. "Did she?" he said. "Then it must be true." He slid back into his seat. "Your daughter has what we call 'a keen eye.'"

"Do you have children, Mr. Hansen?"

"A daughter, as it happens."

"Then you know about the judgments of the young." She nudged Cinda's shoulder. "Come on, babe. We have to go."

Everyone stood.

"I'll walk out with you," Hansen said, and he waited while Fat Alan Dolby, the assistant supervisor, pawed through Cinda's bag for stolen items.

"Talk about breach of trust," Cinda said.

"That's my blue Chevy just across the way." Hansen pointed. The rear license plate read: *Arizona* and, in smaller letters, *Grand Canyon State*, under a picture of the kind of cactus you saw in Road Runner cartoons.

"I thought the Grand Canyon was in Colorado," Cinda said.

"You see," said her mother, "you don't know everything."

"Nobody does," Hansen said. "It was a pleasure meeting you,

Beth." He gave them a small wave and went to the blue car, his bag of groceries nested in one arm.

When they were in the Volvo, Cinda said, "Didn't you like him?"

"He seemed quite personable."

"I think we should invite him to dinner."

Her mother started the engine. "Let's not rush things," she said.

*　*　*

A week later, Edward Hansen was sitting with them at the dining-room table, drinking a white wine spritzer and talking with Mother as if the two of them were old school chums.

"Is it really Beth?" he was saying. "Or is Beth short for Elizabeth?"

"I don't confess this to everybody," Mother said, "but it's short for Bethany."

He looked surprised.

"You mustn't tease me," Cinda's mother said. "Please."

"I wouldn't think of it. Bethany is unique."

"So is Cinda," Cinda said. "By the way."

Not that she felt left out or anything.

"Cinda says you're new in Orlando," her mother said. "Where have you come from?"

"I lived in Phoenix until a few months ago," he said. "Well—Scottsdale, to be precise, but same difference."

"And what brought you here?"

"Mother," Cinda said. "It's rude to pry."

"We're only talking," her mother said. "Nobody's prying."

"And I don't mind the question," Hansen said. "The truth is, I'm not sure why I picked this part of the world. Except there looked to be a lot of possibilities. All the activity at Canaveral—the shuttle launches, the cruises—and what you people down here call 'the attractions'—Disney and Universal and Sea World. You know."

He stopped and looked at his hands, which had short fingernails clipped almost straight across, not curved to follow their natural shape. "And a little bit of nostalgia, too."

"So you'd been here before," Mother said.

"I'd brought Ruby here—my daughter—when she was thirteen. We went to Disney."

Ruby. How lame was that? And he was the one who'd made a thing out of *Cinda.*

"When was that?" Cinda asked.

"Years ago. Twenty plus. The town was a lot different then."

Twenty-plus years ago, she wasn't even on the horizon and her parents weren't married.

"Where is Ruby now?" her mother wanted to know.

"I didn't mean to mislead you," he said. "She's dead."

There was an excruciating silence. Finally, Cinda's mother said she was sorry to hear that; it almost sounded as if she'd had something to do with Ruby dying.

"She was on that flight that blew up over Scotland."

"Lockerbie," Mother said. "I remember. All those people."

Jesus, Cinda thought. The poor man.

"Two-hundred fifty-nine on the plane," Hansen said. "Eleven on the ground."

Details again.

"It must have been dreadful for you," Mother said.

"Excuse me," Cinda said, rising, "but I've got a last-minute term paper to take care of." If this was the gloomy direction the talk was going in, she'd prefer watching television in her room.

* * *

THE NEXT TIME HANSEN came into the EcoMart on her shift, Cinda was on break. Outside the store, on the cement apron between the entrance and the parking lot, were patio tables and metal chairs with mesh seats, and she was sitting alone with a can of Diet Coke she had brought from home. She saw his car as it entered the lot, watched him park between a pair of SUVs that made his Chevy disappear. When he emerged he smiled and headed straight for her.

"Are you malingering?" he said.

She scowled at him. "What's that supposed to mean?"

"Loafing," he said. "Goofing off."

"I'm on break," Cinda said. "It's part of the contract we have with EcoMart. I'm not bending any rules."

"I meant to be joking," Hansen said. "I must be losing my touch."

Cinda took a last swallow from the Coke can and set it aside.

"I think I've got you figured out," she said. "You do some kind of security job. Used to. That's why you ask so many questions."

Hansen looked embarrassed. "Something like that," he said.

"I tried my theory out on Mother. She agreed with me, and she said she hopes you find a situation that suits you."

"Thank you both."

"And we were both of us really sorry about your daughter," Cinda said. "I didn't mean to be rude when I walked out the other day. I just couldn't deal with it at the time."

"I wasn't offended," Hansen said. "I shouldn't even have mentioned Lockerbie. It's my problem, and it was a really long time ago."

"Mother says it was a terrorist bomb."

Hansen looked grim. "That was in the days when they were careless about screening baggage," he said. "Nowadays it's better—a little."

"Mother's taking me to London for Christmas," Cinda said. "It's my reward for escaping high school."

"I haven't been to Britain since eighty-eight," Hansen said. "I had to go over to claim the body. What was left of it."

Was he trying to make her uncomfortable all over again? She hoped he was just talking, just being himself, but how were you supposed to react to somebody else's grief? She really couldn't cope with it.

"You'll have to excuse me," she said. She gathered in her Coke can and stood up. "They only give us ten minutes."

"That's fine," Hansen said. He was smiling again, so it was all right. "I was on my way to the bank. I only stopped off to say hello when I saw you malingering."

"Whatever you want to think," Cinda said. Then she said, "Are you some kind of secret agent?"

Now he laughed. "You know what, Cinda? You pretend to be tough, but you're really a romantic."

*   *   *

OFF AND ON THROUGH THAT SPRING, Edward Hansen was their guest. Sometimes he came for lunch, once in a while dinner; rarely, on lazy afternoons, he would sit by the pool with Cinda and her mother. Mother would make margaritas and serve them in pastel-colored plastic glasses with clear stems. Cinda would drink diet ginger ale and try to get a word in edgewise.

"I don't know if you've noticed," Cinda would say, "but a lot of the people who shop in a health food store don't look particularly *healthy*. I used to think the customers at EcoMart shopped with us because they wanted to improve their health. Now I think maybe eating health food is bad for them, and that's why they look the way they do."

"Chicken and egg," Hansen said. "Which comes first, the health food or the poor health?"

"Exactly."

"I like your mind," he said. "Some investigators would call you cynical. But others would say you're original."

"And what do *you* think, Edward?" Cinda's mother wanted to know.

Hansen smiled. "Original, of course. Like her mother."

Which was the lamest, fakest kind of flattery, but Mother ate it up. She looked forward to Hansen's visits, and usually managed to have a hair appointment the day before he was to stop by.

"I think you're interested in him," Cinda said later.

"He's pleasant company," her mother said. "Not like several men I won't name."

Cinda could name them all, but didn't.

*   *   *

AT ONE OF THEIR POOLSIDE SATURDAYS, it came out that in September Cinda would be studying art and design in Savannah.

"I'm not surprised to find out you're artistic," Hansen said. "It shows up in the way you do your work at the store—your concentration, your poise."

What was all that? His ice-blue eyes were melting all over her, and for an instant her early picture of Edward Hansen as deviant flickered in her mind's eye. Or perhaps he meant to look fatherly, which she thought was slightly worse than being a pervert.

Mother saved the moment. "That remains to be seen," she said. "Especially the 'concentration' part."

"Not to mention the 'poise' part," Cinda added.

"But you must be excited about it," Hansen said.

"Mostly I don't give it much thought. Every now and then I'll stop in the middle of doing something and I'll get this weird, like, *swoosh* in the pit of my stomach—and then I think how different my life is going to be, and how I won't be around the people I've got used to being around." She ducked her head in the direction of her mother. "But I haven't freaked out. Not yet anyway."

"What made you pick Savannah?"

"Cinda's always been a doodler," her mother said. As if that answered the question.

"My art teacher gave me a whole bunch of brochures," Cinda said. "I wrote to half a dozen places."

"She really wanted to go to Chicago—to the Art Institute."

"No, I didn't," Cinda said. "That's where *you* wanted me to go."

Mother gave Hansen her famous helpless look. "I only wanted the best for Cinda."

"Whether Cinda wants it or not."

Hansen laughed and clapped his hands, as if he'd just heard a joke. "You wait, young lady," he began, and Cinda interrupted him.

"If you're going to tell me to wait till I'm a mother myself," she said, "please just don't."

*   *   *

THE WORST TIME WAS THE DAY Hansen and Mother got into a semi-argument about terrorism, and bombs, and airplanes.

"I can't even hear a plane flying over the house," her mother said, "without thinking of 9/11."

Which was a bizarre thing for her to say, because when the wind was from the south, as it often was, the flight path to OIA was right over their pool. If Mother reacted to every plane she heard, she'd never think of anything *except* 9/11.

But Hansen went right along with it. "I know," he said. "I was the same way. Bad images linger."

"I can't tell you how it upsets me," Mother said. "I'll be watching a *Friends* rerun—and all at once there are the twin towers, half their windows lighted up, and I think, 'Oh, dear God.'"

"It's distressing," he said.

"I wish they could go back through all the old TV shows and movies and magazine ads, and somehow *remove* them—the towers—

just edit them out. Make them disappear as if they'd never existed and three thousand people hadn't died in them when they fell."

"But it wouldn't bring any of them back to life."

"I never said it would." Her mother sounded peevish.

"And you know what else?" Hansen said. "Now we can appreciate the others. The Chrysler Building. The Woolworth Building. The Empire State. Those are the real skyscrapers. Those show imagination, and spirit, and beauty, and *splendor*."

Splendor. That was a word you didn't hear much.

"Three thousand human beings, dead," her mother said, as if that was her only point after all. "How can you forget?"

He looked down at his empty margarita glass. "I can't," he said. "But I think when you screw something up, you have to put the best possible face on it."

Cinda sat at the side of the pool and listened. Whenever she looked up at an airplane, she didn't see a second plane exploding into the Trade Center and she didn't think about three thousand people dead. She didn't see a plane filled with college students, thinking they were going to be home for the holidays, not dreaming the world was about to end. She only imagined a couple of hundred seats in coach filled with a bunch of parents—more moms than dads—and bratty kids on their way to Disney World.

"It's all what your generation calls a 'flashback,'" Cinda said. "If you asked me, I'd tell you both to stop watching those re-runs on television."

It seemed a simple enough piece of advice, but that night after she went to bed Cinda lay awake considering the difference between her mother and Edward Hansen. Her mother was upset by a tragedy that truly didn't concern her. She didn't know anybody who had died in the collapse of the Trade Center towers; she didn't even have friends who knew anybody who died there. She was reacting—even though she might be reacting genuinely—to pictures on a television screen.

Cinda had seen the same pictures, though not *live*—she was in English class when it happened—and she had seen commercial flights overhead, sitcom repeats showing landmarks that no longer existed, out-of-date photographs of the New York skyline. But these left her unaffected. Maybe mother's whole life since Daddy divorced her was what was called "vicarious": she felt what happened to others as if it were happening to her.

But it was different for Edward Hansen. It was all *real* for him— explosives and terrorists and the death of people you loved. He had lost his daughter, for God's sake. He'd had to go to Scotland and claim what was left of her body, and fly home with the remains of a woman too young dead, stone cold in the baggage compartment under his feet.

* * *

HE DIDN'T COME TO HER high school graduation—not that she'd really expected he would, not after that weird discussion by the pool. She'd hung on to her last commencement ticket until the day before baccalaureate, and then she gave it to Fat Alan, who seemed genuinely surprised to have it.

When another whole week passed with no sign of Hansen at Eco-Mart, Cinda imagined he might have taken a job with the Homeland Security people—screening baggage, or taking fingerprints, or just looking for terrorists and in-general evil. She wondered if he would always be thinking about the daughter who'd been blown up over Scotland, and whether he used to imagine he might someday come face-to-face with the actual man who'd made the bomb or packed it into the suitcase, or who'd worn the stolen badge of a TWA baggage handler and loaded it onto the plane. And then what? Was that why he'd gone to work as a secret agent in the first place? She didn't know; she couldn't put herself in his shoes.

It was a shame nothing had happened between him and her mother—not that Cinda saw herself as a matchmaker, like one or another of Mother's friends who came around after the divorce and pushed her into the path of some middle-aged man smelling of cigarettes and aftershave. "Listerine breath," her mother would report, "and too many hands." Still, Edward Hansen had seemed a cut above—smart and reserved, and obviously a lonely person. One drawback was that Ruby, if she'd lived, would be almost Mother's age. Another was the possibility of a Mrs. Hansen, assumed to be divorced, but never once mentioned at poolside.

On her last day at EcoMart, Cinda decided to find out the range of the hand scanner she had used for almost a year. It was nearly three months since Hansen had vanished, apparently for good, and though she sometimes expected him to reappear in her check-out lane—more wish than expectation, she admitted to herself—he never did. Now that she was packed for college and ready for Mother to drive her to Savannah, it was likely she would never see him again, but the very first question he asked had stayed with her.

The experiment was a bust. After the last customer had left, and the front doors were locked, she aimed the gun at the magazine display across the aisle—a distance she estimated to be a little more than four feet. Nothing happened; she couldn't even see the thin line of the laser against any product code: not the *TV Guide*'s, not the crossword puzzle booklet's, not even the *National Enquirer*'s. When she leaned out over her counter to cut the distance in half, she thought she saw a red flickering over the *Enquirer*'s UPC, but the scanner didn't register it.

"What are you doing?" Ronnie said. She had come out of the cash-up room, and now she was standing behind Cinda.

"Trying to find the range," Cinda said. "How far away can this thing scan?"

Ronnie laughed. "Eleven inches," she said. "Less than a foot. All you had to do was read the manual in the supervisor's office. You can ask Dolby. 'From two to eleven inches.' I'm quoting."

"That's not very far," Cinda said.

"It's enough. What were you going to do? Play 'Star Wars' with it?"

Which, if the truth were known, wasn't so far off from what Cinda had in mind—not wars, exactly, but competitions among the cashiers. She'd thought they might set up different products at various distances, the more expensive ones farthest away and the cheap ones closer in. Everybody takes a turn, a certain number of scans, and high total wins. At game's end you could clear the register and the supervisor would be none the wiser.

"Don't be silly," Cinda said.

Waiting for her ride home, she amused herself by imagining that when she and her mother went through security on their holiday trip to London, Edward Hansen would be the agent at the checkpoint; then she could tell him about the game, and why it failed. He'd pass the metal-detecting wand up and down and around her, looking for keys and belt buckles and the coins that concerned him so much, and she'd say to him, "What do you suppose is the range of one of those things? How far away can you stand before you can't read me anymore?"

The Tennis Lover

When she came into the room, he was sitting up in the bed nearer the window, two pillows propped against the headboard, the TV remote not far from his right hand.

"So," she said. "Did you watch?"

"Yes. I was sad about the last set."

"I believe it was my worst ever." She slid the bag off her shoulder onto the other bed and sat down beside it. "You believe?"

"Probably one of your worst. There was the Newport fiasco."

"You would remember that."

"Because your bad matches are unforgettable."

"Anyway, that was two years ago almost. I've had many good matches since that one."

He shrugged. "A few."

She showed him a finger. It gave him so much pleasure to tease her. "Bastard," she said. "I've earned enough so we don't starve."

"True."

"And keep you in bourbon."

"Irish," he said. "There's a difference, as I remind you every time the matter arises."

"Whiskey," she said. "It's all whiskey."

"That much is true." He leaned across to the nightstand between the two beds and retrieved the Kent pack. "Why don't you shower and get into your civvies so we can have dinner."

"What is 'civvies'?"

"Your civilian clothes," he said. "The clothes you wear when you're not in your tennis uniform."

She watched him light a cigarette, using the lighter she had given him in Toronto to mark their first year together.

"What I wear for playing tennis is not uniform," she said. "Policemen are uniform. Firemen. Airplane people."

He pointed the cigarette at her. "Shower," he said. "It's already cocktail time."

*　　*　　*

WHEN SHE EMERGED from the shower, the bath towel tucked above her breasts, a smaller towel wrapped around her wet hair, he was sitting in the chair beside the window, putting on his shoes. Beyond the glass she could see the parking lot, and on the far side of the lot an expanse of green lawn enclosed by chain link. It was like looking at a grass court not brought down to scale.

He stood up and came to her, his shoelaces not yet tied. He kissed her.

"You smell clean," he said. He kissed her again, then sat at the edge of the bed to do the laces. "I thought we should eat in the hotel; it's easier than driving around a strange city, looking for a decent restaurant."

"We could ask the desk person for a nice place," she said. "We could hire a taxicab."

He looked up at her as if she had done something wrong. "I know you like to be extravagant," he said, "but you only reached the quarters."

"Is that so bad?"

"Come on," he said. "Dry your hair and get dressed. You must be hungry, and I need a drink."

She took a bottle of nail polish from the dresser and sat on the other bed to paint her toenails. "I believe you don't appreciate me," she said. "How hard I work."

"Of course I do."

"You talk like quarter-finals is no big doing. You try to make my accomplishment smaller."

He watched her while she applied the polish, left foot first. He was keeping a long silence, and she wondered how he would defend himself. Or would he not defend himself?

"I appreciate that you reached the quarters," he finally said. "Don't misunderstand me. But we have higher ambitions, don't we?"

"We have time," she said. "Am I not young?"

"You are," he agreed. "You are indeed young."

"And pretty?"

"Pretty indeed."

"And, as you American men say, a good lay?"

He seemed shocked; she wondered if, by trying to tease him as much as he teased her, she had stepped over a line.

"If that were important," he said, "the world is filled with pretty women who are good lays." He wasn't smiling.

"Forgive me," she said. "I am taking the faults from my bad match and putting them between us."

"But you may be right," he said. Now that she had apologized, now he would play with her. "If the getting laid is important, maybe I should be looking at other young and pretty tennis players. I might go after one of them."

"Who might you go after?"

"I'm not sure. Possibly some tall Russian." He grinned at her. She marveled at how surprisingly boyish he looked when he put on the grin. "Some leggy blonde."

"And why a Russian?"

"Only that there are so many of them."

"Then why did you begin to look at me?" she wondered. "I'm not Russkaya."

"Exception that proves the rule," he said.

"What does that mean?"

"It's a saying. It means that only you are you, and everybody else is Russian."

She pulled the towel off her hair and threw it at him. "Some foolishness," she said.

*   *   *

HE ASKED FOR A TABLE BY A WINDOW. "For the scenery," he said, which she took as a joke. The view out the window was of the hotel's outdoor pool sheltered on two sides by a wall that blocked any possible view. Two small children, a boy and a girl, were splashing each other at the shallow end. A woman—of course their poor mother—reclined in an orange deck chair, holding a paper novel with a title on its cover too small to read from here.

"This was only my second time in the quarters," she said.

"I know. Next time you'll make the semis." He reached across to cover her left hand, just for a moment. "At least."

"You really believe?"

"Of course I do. You know I don't love losers."

"Except the tall Russians with legs."

He frowned. "Not funny anymore."

Only funny if he were the one saying it, but she didn't tell him that. Instead, she waited while he ordered drinks—Irish whiskey for himself, Campari for her, though he always teased her for liking its bitterness.

"People in the room are admiring you," he told her.

"Why would they do such a thing?" she said. "I'm not a somebody." She looked around the dining room. "I don't see any admiring."

"They're embarrassed. They look only out of the corners of their eyes so you can't catch them."

"You always tease me." He did this too often, she thought. It pleased him to make her feel like a child.

"They know you're a famous tennis player," he said. "They wonder why they can't seem to recall your name."

"To be serious," she said when the drinks arrived, "are you proud of me for this week?"

"I'm always proud of you." He raised his glass, touched hers. "You're a strong player, and you keep getting better."

"You never come to the matches. You never see me, as they say it, alive."

"I see you, live, on the television screen. I see your ground strokes and your net play and your terrific volleys just as they happen, just as if I were up in the stands. I marvel at your devastating fuck-you overheads. I hear the noises you make. I see your frustrations. It's the same as being there," he said. "I'm only not able to smell your healthy sweat until you come home to me."

She didn't know to laugh or be angry. "How you put things," she said.

"The point is," he said, "I'm proud of you, whether I'm there or not." He sipped his drink. "Besides, I don't like Boris."

"Who is Boris? I don't know a Boris."

"Your trainer. Your coach."

"Alexei," she said. "Alexei, Alexei, Alexei. Why can you not remember that name?"

"Why can't you remember Irish?"

"It isn't the same. Alexei is a person, and he is important to me and my career."

"I realize his importance. I just don't like him. And he's always around, always appearing, like a bad penny."

"What is that? 'A bad penny'?"

"Somebody nobody likes, but who always turns up where you'd rather he didn't." He gestured toward the dining room entrance. "For example," he said.

She turned, and here was Alexei, just entering, dressed as though clothes were no matter—the worn jeans, the football shirt with the wide stripes, the old soiled Tretorns. When he recognized her, he came over, making a sort of bow to both of them.

"Ten a.m.," he said to her. "We'll work on the serve."

"Yes. I will be on time."

Alexei pointed an index finger at the table and raised an eyebrow.

"Don't worry," she told him.

He frowned and went away, to sit in a corner far away from the scenery.

"You see? A bad penny."

"You make too much out of him," she said.

"And what was he pointing at?"

"The Campari. I am never to drink more than one drink. He calls it a regimen."

"Colonel Boris," he said. He twirled an imagined mustache with his fingers. "The regimental commander."

"And why do you call him Boris?"

"He reminds me of Boris Badenov," he said. "I think it might be the mustache."

"I don't know a Badenov," she said.

"That's because you don't watch enough television," he said. "Badenov is a figure of evil, like what's-his-name."

"You don't like Boris," she said, "because he doesn't like you. I'm being honest."

"I know you are. What's his reason? That you sleep with me instead of with him?"

"He doesn't like you because you smoke cigarettes."

That made him laugh. "And all this time I thought we were rivals for your affections."

"Boris does not like what is called 'second-hand smoke.' He worries about my lungs."

"I worry about them too," he said. "I consider them whenever possible."

She took this as his strange kind of flattery.

* * *

WHEN SHE WAS READY TO LEAVE the room the next morning, he was leaned against the pillows, reading the paper the hotel put under the door and smoking his third cigarette of the day.

"I have to go now," she said.

"How are you getting to the stadium?"

"Alexei is driving." She hunched her bag—rackets, water, towels—to her shoulder. "Are you watching the tennis today?"

"No matches till afternoon. Men's quarters. They don't interest me."

"No blondes?"

He smiled. "No Russians. No long legs."

"What will you do while I am working?"

"What I always do: wait for you to ditch Boris and come back to me."

She hesitated in the doorway. "What is 'ditch'?"

101

"Something old men say." He stubbed out the cigarette. "Tell Boris to drive with care."

"Don't be afraid." She closed the door between them.

Alexei was already in the lobby, sitting in a leather chair near the elevator, his fingers playing a secret music on the chair arm. He stood when she appeared.

"Good morning, Alexei."

He touched her right hand with the fingertips of his. "I was fearful you might be oversleeping."

"Never," she said. When had she ever been so lazy? When had she ever been late for a workout or a match?

He steered her to his car, his hand a light pressure at the small of her back. The car was a white Honda with an orange parking tag hanging from the inside mirror. She slid onto the front seat while he took her bag and held the door for her. He laid her gear on the back seat and came around to the driver's side.

"Did you make love with him last night?" He said this as he started the car and pulled back the shift lever.

"It's nobody's business," she said.

"Perhaps nobody's," he said, "but I see how when you sleep with the boyfriend, the next day you lose a half-step and add two double-faults to your game."

She doubted the truth of that. "It is nobody's business still."

They were in traffic now, and Alexei was silent through two traffic-light stops. Then he said, "Your boyfriend dislikes me."

"It's true," she said. "But he isn't a boy."

"What is his difficulty? Is he jealous because he thinks I'm your lover? Does he imagine we screw in the locker rooms while you make believe to be out on the court?"

She found this funny, a joke, though she didn't say so. If there was a difference between these two men, it was that to Alexei she was first a tennis player, second a woman, while to her lover it was what was called vice versa. How could this not be obvious to anybody?

*   *   *

WHEN SHE CAME BACK to the room it was almost one o'clock. He had gone back to sleep, his head half-buried in the pillows, the newspaper fallen to the floor. The television was on, tuned to a news channel, only there was no sound.

She chose not to wake him. Even after she had showered and dried her hair, she sat for several minutes on the edge of her bed, watching him sleep. He must have been a beautiful young man; now, more than twice her age, he was perhaps rather handsome than beautiful. This afternoon he would need to shave, and he should think soon about having his hair trimmed—just so, just off the collar.

Neither of them had ever mentioned love, except if they were discussing tennis scores, so questions concerning their feelings failed to arise. When she was unhappy, or when like yesterday her own errors had cost her a match, she would sometimes put such a feelings question to herself. She could not speak for him, but for herself she almost always concluded that she was fond of him. *Fond* was a satisfactory English word for what she felt.

She crossed the space between the two beds and leaned to kiss his forehead. This was *fond*, and it woke him, eyes opened, mouth smiling. He put out his hand to draw her toward him until now she was lying against him, her head on his chest.

"Damp hair," he said. "How was practice? Did you excel? Did Boris give you a gold star?"

"I was very good. I served a thousand times, and each was harder and faster than the one before."

"That Boris," he said. "A slave driver."

He slid away from her until he was sitting and reaching for his cigarettes. She fluffed her hair where it had flattened against his chest, waiting while he lighted up, wondering if they would have lunch.

"You remember the motel in Palm Desert?" he said. "Where we had the poolside room?"

"Of course," she said. "After Indian Wells."

"And how, after we'd had enough sun, we came back to the room and lay on the bed together? Not talking. Not fooling around. Just being quiet and close."

"I remember." She thought she hadn't seen him so serious in a long time, perhaps not since the very beginning, when she had no idea who was this older man, and why was he talking to her?

"How the blades of the fan over the bed caught the light reflected off the pool?" He looked at her—that look she liked but never quite understood. "And how the fan blades seemed to slice the light into tiny pieces that shimmered on the walls of the room?"

"Yes." She knew what *slice* meant. *Shimmered*.

"Years from now," he said, "that's what I'll remember—the way the sunlight looked, flickering, dancing, on the walls above our heads."

"And me," she said. "You will remember me, being there beside you."

He took her hand, lifted it, pressed her fingers to his lips. "Until the day I die," he said.

She freed her hand. He was telling her the history of her progress. First the qualifying, then the wild card, then the seeding. So far the quarters. Perhaps one day soon the semis. She bent toward him and kissed his forehead, which had only today become the definition of fondness. By the time she reached a final he would perhaps be too old for her and, she realized now, she would be much, much too good for him.

Six Love Stories

1. Visits

Coming back to the city on the 10:40 bus from Hartford, Laurence Hussey sits next to a window on the driver's side. The window is askew in its frame, just enough open to let in an unpleasantly cold stream of air, and though he tries as the bus is leaving to push the window closed, he fails—the window moves upward easily, but as soon as he takes his hands away it drops open again like a slack jaw. Twice more he tries, then surrenders and sits back to watch the shabby downtown storefronts become shabbier old homes like the one where he has just visited his father. Solemn red brick places with peeling white trim. Sparse lawns barely beginning to green. Buckled sidewalks and sick elms. Anne Street. Asylum Avenue. The chill air hisses through the crack in the window and draws forbidden cigarette smoke toward him from the seat just ahead. He leans so he can see the bus driver's eyes in the rearview mirror, but the driver is not looking back—and even if he were, what good would it do?

"We had a super dinner," says a woman's voice behind him. "The nicest Easter ever."

"Your daughter-in-law cooked?" A second woman. An accent.

"Her nicest meal ever." The first woman sighs and laughs. "In the beginning she wasn't much in the kitchen."

"Nobody is much in the beginning."

Laurence smiles. Perhaps he should take notes; then the next time he goes to see his father he'll have a story to tell. *Dad? There were these two women on the bus. . . .*

"Were you visiting your children for Easter?" says the first woman.

"We don't do Easter," says the second.

The women didn't know each other, he will say to his father. *They were, you know, thrown together by circumstance.* He wishes he had gone across the street from the bus station and bought a paper. He wishes he had thought to bring a book to read. This is not a long trip, but it's boring.

"What did she cook for you, this daughter-in-law?"

"Ham. A beautiful ham."

The traditional, Laurence thinks. What he and his father ordered, yesterday, in the restaurant: ham, with raisin sauce, and mashed potatoes and green beans, Parker House rolls, a little light wine. Wine for himself, not for his father.

"What else?" The woman with the accent—Polish, he thinks now—must be making a list. "A fancy dessert?"

"Yes, but for the moment I can't think what."

An old woman, forgetful. Laurence tries to recall the others waiting at the bus station, several of them women. Which is she, this lady with the faulty memory? Not to be critical—his own memory is beginning to sputter like an old outboard motor, and his father, nearly ninety, can remember in detail all the jobs he held during the Depression, but can't recall what happened yesterday.

He wants to turn and tell the women to talk about something else, something significant, and the desire is just for an instant overwhelming—so that he sees himself rising up from the seat, bending toward them, saying angry words—but then he calms himself and makes his muscles relax, and he thinks: *We'll talk about anything to keep from feeling alone.*

✴   ✴   ✴

THE RESTAURANT WHERE HE HAD TAKEN his father for Easter dinner was on the way to Meriden, a white frame place where they didn't accept credit cards, and where most of the waitresses were older—motherly gray-haired women with opaque stockings and discreet hairnets. How many years had it been since he'd seen hairnets?

"This is a nice restaurant," his father said. "Timothy brought me here once. I think it was my birthday."

Timothy is the son of a friend his father served with in the war.

"I've never been here," Laurence said.

"They serve the best chowder," his father said. "Fish. Clam. Lobster stew."

The Easter before, Laurence had driven his father to the shore—in his father's car, never used because the old man's eyesight had gotten so poor. He had cruised from New London to Niantic to Old Lyme, but it was before the season and many places were closed. They ended up at a Howard Johnson's; his father had ordered lobster stew, then complained for the whole meal about the sparseness of lobster meat. The old man ate slowly, deliberately, filling the spoon too full and letting milk dribble over his chin and onto his shirt front. The white shirt was yellow with age and stained by the fallout of other meals.

"I remember," Laurence said. "Seafood chowders are your favorite."

Their waitress appeared, younger than the others, thirtyish.

"I'll have a bowl of your clam chowder," his father said, "and lots of crackers."

"I'm sorry," the woman told him, "but clam chowder isn't on the menu today."

"Not on the menu?"

"It's Easter. We have a special Easter menu."

Laurence leaned across the table and pointed. "See?" he said. "It's pasted over with the Easter special. Ham and raisin sauce. Choice of vegetable."

"No chowder? Not any kind of chowder?"

"We have pea soup," the waitress offered.

"Why don't you give the special a try?" Laurence said.

"All right."

"And I'll have the same, with the green beans."

The waitress wrote. "Green beans for the other gentleman?"

"Yes," Laurence said. "That will be fine."

He watched the waitress go into the kitchen. Tall, no hairnet, big shoulders that would look wonderful naked.

"Maybe I shouldn't mention this," his father said, "but it looks like you're not wearing your wedding ring."

Laurence made his left hand into a loose fist and looked at it as if he were noticing for the first time that the ring was missing.

"I've gained a little weight," he said. That was true. "It needs to be re-sized."

His father was nodding—a gesture that said *Yes, yes, go on*, not *Yes, yes, I see*. He wondered how well his father could see him, how well he could read the expression on his son's face.

"And anyway, Janie and I have been separated for a while."

"I wondered," his father said. "I thought it might be something like that."

* * *

NOW THE BUS IS IN THE CITY, the high hundreds, making its way through neighborhoods that remind Laurence of war, or natural disaster, or Hell itself. Automobiles abandoned at curbside—stripped, demolished, consumed by old fires. Storefronts with windows cracked or shattered or blackened from within by yellow smoke; display signs with neon lettering torn free, unreadable. Shabby men sit in doorways, presiding over broken glass and garbage and all imaginable litter. Dark children play their stunted games in filthy lots. What did they have for Easter dinner?

"Tapioca," the woman behind him says. "A nice tapioca. She poured cream over it from the Haviland pitcher that used to be my mother's."

*   *   *

"I don't know how to carry on a conversation with the man," Laurence says to his friend Candace. They are sitting in the kitchen of her Stuyvesant apartment. "We have no common ground—I never realized that, until my mother died, and then it slowly dawned on me that I'd always talked to her and never to him. I don't even know why I visit him anymore."

"You have an obligation," Candace says. "He's your father and you love him."

"I suppose."

"You do, don't you?"

"Love him? Sometimes I wonder. I sit in that shabby living room with him and I can't think of a damned thing to say. 'What about the Red Sox this year?' I can't ask about his friends; they're all dead. I can't remind him how much he misses Mother. I'm ashamed to take him out to eat, because I can't bear watching him slobber."

"How old is he?"

"Eighty-seven. He can barely see what's going on in front of him. He eats like an infant."

"Be kind," Candace says. "Here." She gets up from the table and opens the refrigerator door. She wears a green satin housecoat she calls "a wrapper," its hemline halfway up her thighs. "I have something special for us."

"What is it?"

"Fresh blueberries." She sets a bowl between them, an empty saucer for each of them. The blueberries are large, almost black.

"Where do you get fresh blueberries at this time of year?"

"Hothouse," she says.

"I'll bet they're frozen."

"They're fresh. Is this a lovers' quarrel? Are we going to argue over the blueberries?"

"How about sugar?" Laurence says.

"Aren't I sweet enough?"

"No cream?"

"You wash them down with this." Candace stands a bottle of clear liquor on the table, and two cordial glasses. "Raki," she says.

"I've never had it," he says. "Is it like vodka?"

"It's Turkish, and it's more like ouzo. If you put water in it, it turns cloudy."

He pours a little into a glass, sniffs at it, tastes it. It has an edge to it that bites his tongue and leaves his throat chilled. "Wow," he says.

"It'll stir you with desire," Candace says. She comes to his side of the table, puts her arms around his neck and sits in his lap. "But let me help."

He lets her kiss him. She takes off his tie, unbuttons the first three buttons of his shirt and kisses him on the collarbone.

"You realize you only visit me when you feel guilty about your father," Candace says. "That's not very often."

"More often than it used to be," Laurence says. He takes a single blueberry from the bowl.

"Aren't you noticing me?" she says. She leans away from him and tilts his jaw upward so that their eyes meet. "Are we going to enjoy today, or what?"

"Certainly," he says. He raises the cordial glass elegantly to his lips. "No more complaining about the old man. No more picking fights."

He sips. Candace hugs his head to her bared bosom. The raki, cold and sticky, dribbles down his chin.

2. Weights and Measures

She was a sometime fashion model, and once, after she had gone to bed early because the day was unusually warm and she was exhausted by it, she had a dream that disturbed her deeply. She dreamed she weighed the same number of pounds as the number of her lover's post office box. The number was 388.

She got up anyway and made coffee, did her exercises, showered and phoned her mother. Over a second cup of coffee she sat at the kitchen table and pondered doing her nails. The telephone rang once.

"It's me," said her lover's voice.

She pressed the buzzer to unlock the lobby entrance. Then she opened the hall door and waited until she heard the elevator arrive.

"What kept you?" she said. "Did you stop at every floor to ask directions?"

*   *   *

She told her lover about the dream.

"That's plenty of pounds," he said, "three-eighty-eight. You could model tents for L.L.Bean."

"I've sworn off chocolate for good," she told him. "Nothing in excess. Nothing in moderation. Just nothing."

"What are you making for breakfast?"

"It's lunch."

"Brunch, then."

"I thought I'd try a soufflé. The last time you were here I offered you an omelet and then discovered I didn't have any eggs. You recall?"

"I do. Except I was the one who offered to make the omelet."

"The best promises are the ones we don't have to keep," she said. "What you don't know is that Mother called the next afternoon, and I told her about your visit. That is, I told her about not having eggs. She was shocked. Horrified. 'I didn't bring you up to be a poor hostess,' she said. 'How could you not have something so basic as eggs?'"

"I wasn't offended."

"I told her you weren't. 'Men. What do men know?' That's what she said to that."

She began separating the eggs for the soufflé. This was the difficult part; she had always thought so. She broke the first egg and let the yolk wobble in her hand, the white slip through her fingers into a measuring cup. She flopped the yolk into a bowl.

"I've never seen anybody do it that way," her lover said.

"It's the only way I know." She broke the second egg.

"There's something about it that's—I don't know—erotic."

She looked at him; he seemed hypnotized by the bright yolk she balanced in her hand. "Is it obscene?"

"No, no," he said.

She did the third egg. Now that he had obliged her to notice, the yolk warming in her palm and the white dribbling over and through her fingers seemed nearly sexual. She felt her cheeks hot. My goodness, she said to herself, am I actually blushing? A moment later her lover had circled in back of her to embrace her.

"You don't feel like three-hundred-eighty-eight pounds," he said. "Why not forget the eggs for a little while?"

"Have it your way."

She squirmed around for a kiss, holding her hands high to keep from getting him sticky. He kissed her a second time.

"Don't let me forget the recipe calls for four," she said.

*　*　*

MONDAY SHE SLEPT LATE. When she woke up she turned on the bedside radio to listen to the weather forecast. Heat. She hauled the pillow over her head and sighed.

I'm too heavy to crawl out of bed, she told the empty room. I don't really mean that, she reminded herself; it isn't a joking matter.

She got up and switched off the radio, made coffee, then came back to the bedroom to do her exercises. The telephone rang three different times. Once it was her mother. Once it was her agent. Finally it was her lover.

"I miss you," he said. "What are we hatching for the weekend?"

"Oh, very clever," she said. "But I don't have to stand for humor; I know my rights."

"By the way," he said, "I persuaded the post office to change my box number."

"To what?" she said.

"A hundred-six."

She shrieked. "Did you say six or sixty?"

"Six."

"Oh, you darling," she said. "Do you have any idea how much I love you?"

3. THE WORD

On the weekends she stayed with him, the first sound she heard in the morning was the meowing of his cat. The people in the next-door apartment also had a cat, only theirs was put out overnight; his was strictly an indoor cat, black and nearly a dozen years old and just beginning to be fat. The next-door cat always came to its front porch and yowled to be let in. His crouched in the bedroom window, peering down, and the two cats carried on a conversation until the next-door cat went inside.

"It's an aubade," she had said to him one day.

"What's that?"

"A morning-song." She'd turned her face toward him and kissed his neck, feeling the sleepwarmth of him radiating from under the blue sheet. "'Aubade for Two Felines.'"

"What time is it?" He always wanted to know the time, as if time mattered.

*   *   *

SHE'D KNOWN HIM NOW for nearly a year, knew by heart the stories of his bad marriage and worse divorce, and of the lovely house in the country he'd had to forfeit. Of course the stories were all as seen through his eyes, so she took everything he said as if she were a confirmed skeptic. But she was not a skeptic; she was in love with him.

She could never get him to admit that he was in love with her. "I've decided to be fond of people," he said, "but I'm too old to love them."

Sometimes she said, "It's her, isn't it," meaning the ex-wife, meaning to propose that she had soured him on love, meaning to give him an excuse for not again declaring his love for a woman—even if they lived together.

Other times she said, "But I love you; I don't mind saying the word to you," meaning she wished for reciprocity, for mutual declarations, for whatever the idea of *love* really had to do with the two of them.

Whatever way she put it, he changed the subject. She despaired of hearing the word.

*   *   *

ONE DAY EVERYTHING CHANGED. It was his birthday and the champagne they drank for celebration had gone to his head; his eyes glistened and his speech slurred and he would not look at her, but only at the cat asleep in her lap where she sat under the bay window.

"That cat," he said. "He used to be an outdoor cat. Had six acres to hunt, was out most of the time except on really cold days in January. He hunted rabbits and pheasants and field mice, and one day he brought home a rat he must have gotten near a neighbor's trash pile. Birds, bunnies, you name it. He was always bringing his trophies home. That's cats."

"So they say." She held the cat in her lap and listened to the man; she watched his face. Both his words and his demeanor were solemn, intense.

"He's healthy as a horse now, this cat. I only have him at the vet's for his annual shots. But all the years I was married, and we lived on those six acres, and there was all this wonderful hunting for him, he was at the vet's over and over. He'd get into fights—other cats, raccoons, maybe a skunk or two—and his wounds would abscess. He always had to take pills, get shots, have the abscesses lanced. And worms. He was always getting worms, especially tape, from the stuff he ate in the wild."

"Poor kitty," she said, petting the cat's wide brow and stroking its tattered ears.

"You pay a price for being free," he said. Now he looked at her. "I think I've finally learned that."

She felt the old cat purring under her hands. *Ah*, she thought, *so this is how he says it.*

4. PILLOW TALK

It was three in the morning and though Quentin had dozed fitfully since coming to bed at eleven, he had not been able quite to relax, quite to fall calmly into sleep. His head ached; the muscles of his neck throbbed; if he lay just so, it felt as if he had pinched a nerve in his left shoulder, and the pain careered down his arm to the elbow. He turned over from his right side to his left and tried to arrange his legs around the cat, curled at the foot of the bed.

"For heaven's sake," his wife said hoarsely, "what's the matter?"

"Nothing," he said. "My legs ache."

"Then take a couple of aspirin."

"Maybe I will."

He put his arms around the pillow and hugged it against his face. He tried not to move, he tried not to be aware of his body. For a while he watched the red pulse of the digital alarm clock, until its numbers changed from 3:23 to 3:24. Then he closed his eyes and thought how even though he had come home nearly two years ago, he might never again be comfortable in his wife's bed.

*　*　*

THE NEXT MORNING he made a phone call. It was not a thing lightly done; he had weighed its advisability during this morning's shower, and rehearsed his lines to the bathroom mirror while he shaved. Now, listening to the telephone's tuneless ring, he was afraid. He rested the fingers of his free hand against the cradle, thinking: If it's a man, I'll break the connection. And then: Or if she sounds hurried.

"Hello." A woman's voice.

"Jan? It's Quentin."

Though he had not hung up, for several moments the silence at the other end of the line nearly persuaded him that she had.

"Quentin," she said finally. Grudgingly. "Look, this isn't a good time. I've got company coming for lunch. . . . "

"I have a favor to ask," he said. "Really, I won't keep you."

"You *couldn't* keep me," she said. "What's the favor?"

"I thought perhaps we could have a drink together, sometime this week." It was not one of the lines he had rehearsed.

"What for? Old times?"

"It's been a couple of years."

"It seems like only forever," she said. "It seems like something that never happened."

"But what do you think?" he said.

"No; forget it." How quickly the impatience rose in her voice. "Damn it, Quent, don't keep calling me like this."

"I don't," he said. In fact, he had called her four times. Once he had gotten her out of the shower, twice he had waked her up, once —he was almost certain—he had interrupted lovemaking. "It's just that I call at bad moments."

"Well this is another," she said.

"Janice." He said the name desperately. "I want my pillow."

"Your what?"

"That's the favor. That's the reason I called. I don't want to have a drink with you—I mean, I'd like to have a drink with you, but it's not why I telephoned. I want my pillow."

"What on earth for?"

"I'm having trouble sleeping."

"Take a pill," Janice said.

"No, really. I can't get comfortable; my neck gets all twisted and stiff."

"This is screwy. You're honestly giving me grief over a pillow that's been on my bed from the beginning?"

"We bought it together," he said. "Remember? We went to Dayton's; I picked it out and charged it to my account."

"I inherited that pillow when I left you," Janice said. "It's mine."

"I slept on it for almost two years," he said.

"You," she said. "Only you could be emotional about a pillow."

"It's nothing to do with the emotions. My neck misses it, my head misses it, my spine misses it. Is there a real reason I can't have it? I'm not asking for the pictures, I'm not asking for the tapes, I'm not asking for the wine glasses. I'm not even asking for the Chicken Wellington recipe."

Janice sighed. "Quent, I don't have the time for this. All right, you can have the pillow."

"Can you meet me at Chase's around four?"

"Carrying a pillow?"

"Please," he said. "We can have a drink, too. We can talk a little."

"Pillow talk," she said. "I always wondered what that meant."

*　*　*

"Do you have any idea what a fool I feel?" Janice said. "Prancing through the streets with a pillow under my arm? Having to walk past those threadbare old men huddled in doorways? You can imagine how they watched me."

"Wistfully," he said.

"Yes." She sat across the table from him with the pillow in her lap. "Just your sort of look."

"You could have put it in a paper bag."

"It's queen-size. Where was I supposed to find a big-enough bag?" She glanced around the room. "Everybody's staring," she said.

"You could sit on it," he said. "I could tell the waiter you're my daughter."

She glared. He had forgotten her killing look, the one that had always told him what a trial he was. He was obliged to avert his eyes and consider the pillow in her lap; the small blue flowers of the ticking reminded him of Saturday mornings—English muffins, love, lugging the clothes hamper to the laundry room, changing the linens of the wonderful bed.

"Do you still drink daiquiris?"

"Sometimes."

"I mean would you like one now?"

"All right." She opened her purse and took out several crumpled bills.

"Let me," he said.

"No. I'll fend for myself."

"Please." He pushed the bills toward her.

"Damn it," she said, "I'm trying not to make a big deal out of this. Do you mind?"

"Sorry."

"This is the second episode we've had over your dumb pillow. Let's make it short, and as sweet as possible." She tried to draw her chair nearer the table; the pillow was in her way. "Here," she said. "Take this thing."

He put it on the floor, propped by the legs of his chair. For a peculiar instant he wanted to hug it, put his face against it.

"What was the first episode?" he said.

"You truly don't remember?"

"Truly."

"About two months after you came back to the States? God, you were in tears. You made me promise to give the pillow to the Salvation Army. You wanted me to swear that no new lover's head would lie on your precious pillow; you said you couldn't bear the thought of it. You assumed that of course I had a new lover—which I did not." She sipped her drink; her tongue attended to the grains of salt on her upper lip. "You don't remember all that carrying on?"

"I do now," he said.

"You are so sentimental," she said. "So maudlin."

"How come you broke your promise? About donating the pillow to the Salvation Army?"

He tried to meet her killing eyes squarely.

"How come you're still married?" she said.

5. FATHERS

"Why don't we forget about the ball," the young woman said. "Why don't you just take a drop?"

The man, considerably older, was in the short rough just off the seventh fairway. He was walking carefully, looking down, swinging the head of a two-iron across the tops of wild flowers.

"It's a Titleist," he said.

"It's not as if you couldn't afford a new one."

"You just want to add a stroke to my score."

"You won't break forty anyway," she said. "Take a drop."

"I can maybe break eighty if we play a second nine." He rested the club on his shoulder and looked broodingly into the scrub pine that separated the seventh fairway from the sixth. "You suppose it's in there?"

"I haven't a clue. You hooked it so badly I couldn't follow it."

"I sliced it," he said. "After all this time I should think you'd know the difference."

"There isn't any difference," she said. "Either way, you can't find the ball."

"You should learn to tell a hook from a slice," he said.

"Maybe you ought to play one of those new orange balls," the young woman said. "It might be easier to find."

"I couldn't," he said. "It would be like knocking a tangerine around the course." He came back toward her, still carrying the club on his shoulder. "Maybe I'd better take a drop," he said. "I don't suppose there's any point in hanging around here all day."

* * *

THE SEVENTH GREEN WAS AT THE TOP of a broad hill, trapped on both sides and at the back. From the foot of the hill where the man's fourth shot had landed, the flag was hidden, and he stood for a long time pondering. His golf bag—plaid, its leather trim badly scuffed—lay on the fairway behind him.

"What do you think?" he said.

"I think it's to the left and toward the back of the green." She sat on the grass nearby, pulling her crossed ankles under her. "If I were the pin, that's where I'd be."

"I mean do you think a seven-iron or what?"

"Seven or eight."

He stooped to haul the iron out of the bag. "Seven," he said. "I don't think I can reach with an eight."

"Not unless you hit it squarely," she said.

He addressed the ball, which lay in a dark green patch of clover. After a few moments of settling his feet, dancing the club head behind the ball, assessing the long sweep of the hill, he straightened up and stepped back.

"I think I'll go take a look," he said.

He trudged up the slope, the club in his right hand. The grass was green to the eye, but down near the soil it had a brownish cast and felt brittle underfoot. He climbed until he could see the flagstick, the flag made of stiff red plastic with a white numeral; it was set in the back left corner of the green, about ten feet in from the frog hair.

He stood, leaning on the club, and looked back down the hill to his ball. The young woman waved; she wore bright yellow shorts and a white blouse, and her hair was held back from her face with a narrow yellow headband. The ball was a white dot not far from her bare legs. It looked like an eight-iron shot after all.

* * *

WHEN THE BALL DROPPED over the rim of the hole, it rattled in the cup with a sound like crockery in a dishwasher. The woman fished it out and tossed it back to him. Then she reset the flag and followed him off the green.

"Double bogey," he said. "I'll be lucky to come in with a fifty."

"Think of the fresh air you're getting," she said. "Think of the dew on the greens and the nice exercise."

He hitched the bag onto his shoulder. "You really don't like this game, do you?"

She shrugged.

"Next time why don't you rent some clubs and try it yourself? If you started to enjoy it, I could buy you a set of your own."

"Maybe," she said. She held out her hand to him. "Here, this is for you."

"What is it?"

"A four-leaf clover. I found it down the hill."

He took it, looked at it, put it carefully in the pocket of his shirt.

"Thank you," he said. He reached out to draw her against him and kissed her on the forehead. "Let's just do the nine holes and call it a day."

* * *

THE EIGHTH HOLE WAS A PAR THREE, a hundred and ten yards from the high tee to a green nested in a natural bowl. The hole was trapped all around. There was scarcely any fairway; instead, the steep hill was sandy and rocky, as if in a permanent state of disrepair. Because the green was invisible from the tee, the young woman had been sent down the hill, and now she stood at a halfway point so that if the ball caromed, or buried itself, or went far off-line, she could keep it in view. She positioned herself beside a dead oak and waited. The man appeared above her, standing at the lip of the hill, shielding his eyes against the sun.

"You ready?" he called.

"Ready," she answered.

He stepped out of sight. After a short time she heard him call out "Fore," and heard the whack of the club head. In the same instant she saw the ball; it was hit short, and landed in the rough just above her, but it was moving at great speed and bounced past her toward the green. A little farther downhill it struck something solid—a large rock, an old stump, she could not tell—and took renewed flight. It landed just at the edge of the green, danced toward the hole, and struck the flagstick straight on. She watched the ball vanish into the cup.

"Did you see where it landed?" The man had found a path from the back of the tee, down through the trees to where she stood. "Am I in trouble?"

"It landed about there," she said, pointing at the hillside.

"In all those damned rocks," he said. "Wouldn't you know it. Did it ricochet?"

"Straight toward the green."

"Thank God for small favors," he said. He started downward, lugging the bag like a valise. "Tell me how far."

She followed after. "You'll be surprised," she said.

"I'll bet." He stood at the front of the green, looking down into the trap. "Where is it?"

"In the hole," she said.

"Don't tease me."

"No, really."

He laid the bag down and walked to the hole. He reached in alongside the pin and took out the ball.

"You put it there," he said.

"How could I?"

He studied the ball. "It actually went in? It's actually a hole-in-one?"

"Actually," she said. "It wasn't the most wonderful shot I ever saw—it must have hit every rock on the hill coming down—but it did the job."

"What do you know," he said. Abruptly, he turned away from the young woman and flung the ball with all his might at the tops of the trees behind the green. She took this to be an expression of joy.

* * *

"WHEN I STARTED PLAYING GOLF, I had to use my father's clubs," he said.

They were sitting over drinks in the clubhouse. The decision to stop at nine holes was sound; he had gone over the last green with a clumsy pitch, then three-putted, and he took his failure at the ninth as an evil portent. With a decent pitch, he would certainly have made par.

"The clubs had funny names: *mashie, niblick, brassie.* You didn't call them by number. It was as if they had distinct personalities. And they were wooden-shafted. The heads were held on to the shafts with this heavy winding of gutta percha twine, and the whole club was varnished to a fare-thee-well."

"What kind of wood?"

"I don't know," he said. "Something resilient. Hickory? You could feel the wood sing when the club head made contact. And the shafts weren't really true; they all had a bow in them. You felt like W. C. Fields playing billiards."

The young woman smiled. "And did you wear knickers?" she said.

"No," he said. "But I went in for argyle socks and sweaters." He pondered the scorecard open beside his Collins glass. "Forty-six, even with the eagle on eight," he said. "Can you imagine it?"

"Did your father teach you the game?"

"After a fashion. He wasn't much of a golfer, I'm afraid—though it took me a while to realize just how bad he was. I think he learned his swing from watching baseball."

"You're quite a good golfer," the young woman said. "In spite of him."

"How one generation resists the faults of another," he said. "Anyway, it's an old man's game."

"Nonsense. You're not old."

He took a last wistful look at his scorecard.

"Who's going to believe this ace?" he said.

The young woman took up both his hands and kissed them gently.

"I am," she said. "Who else do you need?"

6. WEDDING DAY

It was Benjamin Howard's wedding day, the second of his life and, he hoped, the last. Annette, the bride-to-be, was asleep in the bed he had just left; her two daughters were in the kitchen, quarreling amiably over the last blueberry muffin. The orange cat dozed on the picnic table outside the sliding door of the bedroom, mandarin-like, forepaws folded under. Above and beyond the cat, the family mockingbird—he considered it a part of the house rental—was singing from a braided-wire cable that cut the backyard diagonally in half. The cable, coated with a patina of light rust, was a dog-run; the leash was still in place although the dog had died long ago, and every morning around six the mockingbird alighted and began its repertoire. The repertoire was considerable and impressive, and it had grown wider in recent days. This was late May, and Ben imagined the bird's singing had gained new breadth from its recent mating. Over a period of three weeks there had been a flurry of contention between two of the neighborhood's several mockingbirds, and now the fighting had ceased. *The world's in love*, Ben thought.

He padded down the long hall in his bare feet and poked his head into the kitchen.

"I'm taking a shower," he said. "Nobody run water." Not that women ever listened to him, no matter their ages. By the time he finished his shower, the water pressure had dropped off on three occasions, and each time the temperature had wavered between scalding and freezing.

Toweling off, shivering, in the middle of the bathroom, Ben heard the mockingbird going strong: trills, chirps, warbles, riffs that broke off just before they became melodies, successions of joined notes that sounded like the double- and triple-tonguing he had learned when he played trumpet in the high school band. He marveled at the bird's skill, and thought he understood its impatience, its refusal to stick to one song.

In the bedroom, Annette was still asleep—or feigning. She had waked him at three in the morning for love; now she had gone back to pursue her postponed dreams.

He pulled on his underpants. "Anthrax," he said. "Up and at 'em."

"Mmph," she said, motionless and out of sight.

"Come on," he said. "Today's the day we make each other honest." He sat beside the covers where she was buried, leaned over and kissed a barely exposed ear. She smelled of warmth and of sex that crept out from under the sheets like a fog, and he remembered the a.m. perfume of their lovemaking peeling off him and swirling down the shower drain.

"Go away," she said. "Today's my wedding day."

"So I've heard."

"You'd better put your clothes on," she said. "God knows what the groom-to-be will do if he finds you hanging around."

He slid his arms under the bedclothes and caressed her in vulnerable places. "Something like this?"

"Oh, God," Annette said, opening to him. "Be sure the door's closed."

The daughters' voices were far away and sounded like the language of a different country. Coming back to the bed he heard the mockingbird singing on and on and on, trying out everything.

Petra

In the middle of the afternoon, long after the photographs and the volleyball, Petra missed her husband. He was not in the parlor with the grand piano, where some of the uncles and cousins were laughing over a family anecdote she recognized—by the names it contained—as one she had heard at earlier reunions, nor did she see him when she looked out the bay window of the dining room onto the side lawn where the children had just begun the croquet. Not that she was surprised by his absence—it was habitual with him at some point in the annual visit to the farm at Harpswell to drift away from this abundance of relatives to recover himself, "to relax and regird," he told her. One year he had taken the car to the marina at Basin Point and sat for an hour in the small, paneled restaurant, drinking coffee and smoking one cigarette after another until he ran out and chose not to buy a fresh pack. The first reunion he had ever brought her to, he left her with his cousin Steff for Stephanie— and jogged all the way to Bailey's store and back, stumbling into the front hall red-faced and drenched in perspiration. The worst time— last year, it was—she had found him upstairs in what had been his mother's bedroom, sitting in the wicker chair under the window, pale and hypertense, breathing like some beached sea creature. Now she poked her head into the kitchen.

"Has anyone seen Donald?"

Three women lifted their faces toward her. Two of them looked blank. The other, Aunt Louisa, shook her head.

"That man," Aunt Louisa said. "He's predictable as tides."

Petra went out to the croquet match. "Has anyone seen your Uncle Don?" she said.

No one had.

* * *

SHE FOUND HIM, FINALLY, in the family burial ground in the overgrown pasture far behind the house. He was sitting near its center, his suitcoat folded under his rump like a stadium cushion, his necktie looped untied around his neck, his chin resting on his cradled knees. He was staring at the family monument, a large blue-granite stone in a shape resembling a chair-back.

"I wondered where you'd got to," Petra said. "Are you okay?"

"Sure."

"I thought you might have decided to jog to Brunswick and back."

He smiled slightly. "Too hot," he said.

"Well. I just wondered what was up."

"I couldn't remember what year my grandmother died," he said. "I keep telling Aaron—" Aaron was his therapist "—that my mother left my father the year my grandmother died, and he keeps saying: 'What year was that?' and I can never tell him."

"What year was it?"

"See for yourself; 1945."

"Does it help?" She sat carefully on the browned grass and arranged her seersucker skirt over her knees. "Does it all come back to you?"

"No," he said. "Is that sarcasm?"

"Certainly not." Though she was not entirely sure: It might very well have been sarcasm. More and more her true response to her husband's search for himself, his past, lay somewhere between indifference and impatience. When he started it, nearly five years ago, she had encouraged it, as if it were a quest—as if Donald were a medieval knight, and she the earnest damsel whose token he wore. Now . . . in the thirsty grass under her hands she found a single green weed, a small yellow flower blossoming out of it. She uprooted it, examined its petals.

"I was twelve years old," Donald said. "It baffles me that I can't remember; it isn't as if I was an infant."

"It sounds like something you don't want to remember."

"I know that," he said irritably. "I'd just like to know what's so damned awful about it. Why have I buried it so?"

Petra had no answer. She let her eyes stray to the family monument—that ugly granite lump; it was hard to imagine such bad taste in a thing so important. At her first-ever reunion Donald had brought her here and she had walked around it, reading the names of his grandparents, their brothers and sisters, the birth and death dates. The list hadn't changed; his mother's name was still missing, though she had been dead for seven years.

"Did they have a fight?" she said. "Did they break the crockery and swear and hit each other?"

"No," he said. "There was never anything like that. Just words."

"No cursing at all?" Not like us, she wanted to say.

"A damn or a hell was extreme for them both. When my dad was really furious with me, he'd say something like 'What the deuce is the matter with you?' That was one step up from 'What the dickens . . .'" He stood and picked up his suit jacket. "Let's go back," he said.

He extended his hand; she got to her feet without its support.

"What about your grandmother?" she said. "Were there scenes? Between her and your mother? Between her and you?"

Donald dusted off his jacket and carried it over his shoulder as they walked toward the farmhouse.

"She was savage enough," he said. "But there weren't what you'd call outbursts. She was very tough on my mother. Mother was a kind of servant in the house, I realize now, but Nana applied a constant pressure, a relentless force of will. It was her house, after all. My mother was always off balance because of that; she had no place to stand and resist."

"If you remember that sort of conflict, I don't see why you can't remember everything. That's pretty subtle for a twelve-year-old."

He stopped and slipped into the jacket. It was his pale blue Palm Beach, and Petra noticed it had a tiny grease spot on one of the lapels. He saw it, too, and dabbed at it with one finger. They were standing at the back door of the shed.

"Damn you, Petra. The whole point is that I don't remember all that." He followed her into the cool darkness of the shed, into the smell of old wood and of cut weeds moldering on the blades of mowing tools. "Most of what I know about those days comes from Aunt Louisa."

"Don't curse me," Petra said. "Why don't you just send Aunt Louisa to Aaron and be done with it?"

* * *

A WEEK EARLIER PETRA HAD MET HER FRIEND Susan for lunch at a Lebanese restaurant in the East Thirties. The weather was oppressively hot; a single ceiling fan turned above their heads, making a token disturbance in the heavy air.

"At least I've got the packing done," she told Susan. "I don't have to go home to more of that."

"Should we get more wine?" Susan said.

"Not for me. Not in this heat."

"But you must be looking forward to it just a little. Aren't you? Good lord, it's Maine. You'll be out of this hot-box city."

"It's such a love-hate thing," Petra said. "I love the family manse. It's a big old rambling house with high ceilings and pine floors, and lightning rods at the roof peaks, and hundred-year-old lilac trees outside the front door. And the setting—a meadow of wild flowers, and a blueberry field, and from the upstairs windows you can see the ocean." She poked at her food with a fork. "I don't know why I keep coming here," she said. "I hardly ever know what I'm eating."

"If somebody invited me up to Maine," said Susan, "I'd say yes in a minute."

"I always go with him," Petra said. "And it's down to Maine, not up."

"Down, then."

"But poor Donald—it sends him into such a spin. He's bad enough in the city, it offends him so and he so needs to escape to someplace where he can breathe. He drives me up the walls; I can't stand being used that way. I can't bear having to mother him, to put up with his depressions, to be continually patient with him. I've finished with all that; I've raised my kids and booted them out into the world, and now I want to tend to myself. You know?"

"I know."

"So I want Donald to go home to the sun and the seagulls and that lovely salt air. But what that family does to him . . ."

"I don't see why you can't go to Maine without going to the annual reunion," Susan said.

"Oh, God," Petra said. "Picture that. He'd accuse me of cutting him off from his roots."

"Tell him it would be a good thing."

"No, he's got a passion for finding out who he is, and what he is; it's the one passion he has left."

"You should tell him that if he finds out too much, he'll let the past dictate the present. Tell him it's better to live without intentionality."

Petra studied her. "I don't think that's true," she said. "And anyway, I couldn't tell him such a thing. I couldn't knock the props out from under him."

"Then suffer," Susan said.

"Thanks."

"The fact is: I think you pussyfoot too much around Donald's precious ego. I think you ought to leave him and have it over and done with."

"I don't know. Maybe I ought to. Maybe one day I will."

"What did we decide?" Susan said. "More wine or not?"

* * *

THE KITCHEN SMELLED OF STRING BEANS. They were heaped on a table top whose porcelain veneer had begun to wear away to the black metal underneath. Aunt Louisa was snapping the beans into short lengths, an aluminum saucepan cradled in her lap to hold them. Petra sat across the table, drinking iced tea. She felt her presence had interrupted something significant, but she had given up staying away; for a half-hour she had borne with a cousin's discussion of cemetery plots and perpetual care. Donald was hunched over the back of a chair in which he sat the wrong way, rubbing idly at one of the spots worn through the porcelain.

"When I was small, I used to think these were flies," he said.

"How small?" Petra asked.

"Four, five, I guess. An age when I didn't understand the difference between animate and inanimate. It was a great mystery to me: Why didn't these flies ever leave the table?"

"He used to slap at them," Aunt Louisa said. "When he was older he tried to fill in the spots with mashed potato."

"Did I really?" Donald said.

"Always the perfectionist," Petra said. She sipped from the humid tumbler. The smell of the tea mingled with the smell of the string beans. The summer before, Petra had helped; she remembered the moist, shiny cross-section where the beans broke, and the tiny white seeds inside the pods.

"Oh, Donnie was a sketch," Aunt Louisa said.

Donald looked sidelong at Petra and winced.

"He spent every summer here, at least a month. He and Stephanie would go down at low tide to dig for quahogs, and splash around after mussels in the tidal pools . . ."

Petra felt her attention drifting away. Now Aunt Louisa would ask Donald if he remembered when she raised collie dogs; did he remember the old Chevrolet; did he remember the Fourth of July when his Uncle Frank set off a stick of dynamite in Tom Bibber's potato field? Oh, Donald, she wanted to say, you're not digging any deeper. You're only moving back and forth over the same old ground. I've heard your past so many times, I almost believe it's my own.

She bowed her head and rested the cold glass against her forehead.

"But when was that?" she heard Donald say. "When did my mother do that?"

"I don't know," said Aunt Louisa. "It might have been just after the war. Or—no, the war was still going on."

She brushed a wisp of hair out of her eyes. "It was so long ago, Donnie. You mustn't trust my poor recollection."

"But I don't remember anything about it," Donald said. "Just tell me what you think was happening."

"Well . . ." She carried the saucepan to the sink and ran water into it, then set it on the back of the stove. "You know it was never much of a marriage," she said.

"I knew there was a problem because they were living in Nana Lowe's house."

"That was part of it; no doubt of that. My sister was a strong woman, a willful woman, and she and your father's mother were at it hammer and tongs most of the time." She sat at the table and poured herself a glass of tea. "If the truth were known, Sarah Lowe was not a likable person. So I believed most of what your mother was telling me in those days."

"Why did she leave Father?"

"There was an ultimatum. Annie told him she was fed up with being a servant to his mother, of being ordered around in the kitchen, of being treated like a poor relation. She told him she was moving out, lock, stock, and barrel, and if he wanted his wife and son back he had better find a home she could call her own. That was all there was to it."

"And she came here."

"She came here, and you and she took over the front room. She clerked at Bailey's for a while, and then she clerked in Brunswick, at Senter's store." Aunt Louisa put her tea aside and wiped her hands on her apron. "Annie paid her way while she lived here. She always paid."

"How long were we here?"

"Oh, all summer. From late spring almost until fall—I remember there was some talk about you going to school here, and a visit to Harold Cole, who was on the school board in those days."

"But that didn't happen?"

"No, you went back to Scoggin, Labor Day weekend. Your father'd rented an apartment. 'God bless him,' Annie said, 'he does love me.'"

Aunt Louisa sighed as if what she remembered had just taken place. "That's as may be," she said. "At least it postponed the divorce by ten years."

"But there was nothing else special about that summer?" Donald said.

He looked desperately at Petra, who thought: He wouldn't even mind if she made something up. Aaron wouldn't mind, either.

"It was a nice summer," his aunt said. "Your mother did a lot of gallivanting, looking up old school chums. You and I had a few special times while she was gone."

"Did we?" he said.

"We'd go down to the Point and climb on the rocks and look for sailboats. Sometimes we'd pack a picnic lunch. You used to peel my hard-boiled egg for me—Lord, you were so slow and so deliberate about it—and we'd talk."

"That's funny," Donald said.

"You'd ask me the darnedest questions," Aunt Louisa said. "How old was your mother? Why didn't Cousin Stephanie like you?—but she always did, you know. Where was your daddy? Why didn't you have a sister?" She stood up from the table and repositioned a bone hairpin in her hair. "But I can't carry on like this," she said. "I've got all those mouths to feed. You two go along."

"Could I ask just one question?" Petra said. "Why isn't Don's mother's name on the family gravestone?"

Aunt Louisa appeared surprised.

"Why," she said, "I really don't know. I guess no one ever got around to making the arrangements."

* * *

WHEN SHE CAME UPSTAIRS after helping the other women with the supper dishes, Petra found Donald face down on the brass bed. He was in his shirtsleeves; the Palm Beach jacket hung scarecrow-like on a bedpost. The sunset cast long shadows from the gable window onto the far wall.

"Are you asleep?"

"No." He didn't move, and the word muffled itself in the pillow.

Petra sat on the edge of the bed. "How old do you think Louisa is?"

"I don't know." He turned his face toward her. "She's got to be late sixties, maybe early seventies."

"How come she never got married?"

"How the hell do I know?" He reburied his face and hugged the pillow.

"Tonight after supper she was talking a lot about your father. Did she used to have a thing for him?" Petra slipped off her shoes and pulled her legs up onto the quilt. "Did you know your father courted her before he finally decided to make your mother miserable instead?"

Donald rolled onto his back. "You have a way with words," he said.

"Why didn't you remind Louisa that your mother moved back home because your Nana Lowe conveniently died?"

"Tact," he said. "Good old-fashioned tact."

Petra slid off the bed and went to the curtained closet. She took her blue nightgown from its hook.

"I like this room," she said. "I like the old maps on the walls, and that old treadle sewing machine under the window."

"It's charming."

"It must mean a lot to you—this old house."

"It means something."

"What's the matter?" she said. "If you don't want to talk to me, just say so."

"I was remembering," Donald said.

She unclasped her earrings and laid them on the dresser. "Is it a breakthrough?" she said. "Is it something to tell Aaron?"

"Aunt Louisa told me I murdered my sister." He looked at Petra. "Can you imagine?"

She couldn't. She wanted to say: You don't have a sister. But she said: "Today? She told you that today while I was planning the hereafter with your cousin Bartlett?"

"Before," he said. "That summer she was talking about, when she used to take me down to the Point and I asked all those questions. One afternoon she told me that if I hadn't been such a difficult birth, my sister wouldn't have been stillborn."

"That's cruel," Petra said. "Even if it's true, it was a cruel thing to say to a—what? A twelve-year-old."

"I'd forgotten it." He turned away from her and wrapped his arms around the pillow. "Totally forgotten it."

"Don't make too much of it; let it stay forgotten."

"I can't."

"You've done it for years," she said. "There's nothing gained by brooding over it now."

"Nothing for you," Donald said.

She watched herself in the dresser mirror, a woman in evening shadow taking off a white blouse. "Let's sleep," she said. "We've got a long drive tomorrow."

*　*　*

PETRA LAY IN THE DARK knowing Donald was still awake, his mind pivoting on the discovery of the day, the revived memory he would carry back to the city. Souvenir of Maine. How these family visits stimulated his quest. Or his invention—she could never quite be sure.

She propped herself on one elbow and smoothed the pillow into a different shape. The small spine of a goose feather pricked her finger; she worked it out through the weave of the pillowcase and put it aside. She imagined it floating to the floor, lodging invisibly between wide pine boards.

"Can't sleep?"

"Speak for yourself," Petra said.

"Now can we talk?"

"If you want." She lay on her right side, to face him.

"What would you think about getting away from each other for a while?" Donald said. "Separating."

"Because you murdered your sister?"

"Don't," he said. "It isn't funny."

"Then why?"

"Because I obviously have more things to learn about myself. Because, just as obviously, I upset you in the process."

"Have I complained?" Petra said.

"You don't have to. I can read you—your discontent."

She bent the pillow double and sat up against it. "You can't even read yourself," she said. "Are we talking divorce?"

"I don't know."

"Then what happens? I go back to the city by myself, and you stay on with the family?"

"Something like that."

"Let me think about it," Petra said.

She leaned her head back against the brass uprights of the bedstead and listened. She heard the sea, far off through the pine trees; she heard the wind in the old shutters; she heard her own heart. She thought: Never mind all the times I've wished to be away from this man. It frightens me, the prospect of living alone.

"'You cracked your mother open like a walnut,'" Donald said. "That's what Aunt Louisa told me on the rocks that day."

"My good God," Petra said. "Will you let up?" She clenched her fists in her lap. "Spare me all the secret-keepers of your life—your sainted mother, your wicked Nana. . . ." She stopped herself, amazed at her anger.

Donald was silent.

"It kills me, what you expect from us," she said.

"Who's 'us'?"

"Women. Wives. Me." She hugged her bare arms. "When I think of your mother," she said, and let her voice fall.

"What?" Donald said. "What about her?"

"How she wanted me to stay with you, no matter what. She made me promise it."

"When was that?"

"The day before she died," Petra said. "On her death bed." *Emphasis.*

She sat upright and turned on the lamp. Donald was staring at the ceiling; he was frowning, and his jaw was set.

"I cannot believe my mother would do that to me," he said after a while.

"Do what?"

"Bind me to marriage. Oblige me to hold on to a thing that destroys me."

"Is that what Aaron tells you? That your marriage to me is destroying you?"

"No, of course not." He drew the hem of the sheet up as a shield against the light. "Of course Aaron doesn't tell me that."

"Then what?"

"He doesn't tell me anything. He asks. He keeps urging me to work things through."

"I'd like to know what Aaron thinks holds me," Petra said, "and whether I'm being destroyed, too." She thought of the relatives, the cousins and uncles and aunts, the croquet-playing children who reminded her how she had ceased to be a mother when her own children left home for college and the army. What marriage had done since then was burden her with lists of names she had at last managed to memorize, to put faces to, and now Donald had decided to want a divorce. "Is it your mother who's breaking us up?"

"No," he said. He turned onto his side, away from her.

"You're not trying to follow in her footsteps?"

"Leave my mother out of this," he said.

"You make me sick," Petra said. "You imagine every woman in the world is hiding some special knowledge that you need in order to understand yourself."

"Maybe I do," he said. "What of it?"

"But the truth is that the difference between men and women isn't a matter of what we know, but when we know it. Your mother's Caesarean was nothing unusual; it's no fault of yours that she was torn up by having you."

"I'm happy to hear it."

"The thing about women is: When we're hurt, we feel the pain right away—not thirty or forty years afterward."

"I suppose that means I'm insensitive?" Donald said.

His flippancy irritated her. "No," she said. "Just damned earthworm slow."

* * *

WHEN SHE WOKE UP LATER it was beginning to be daylight, and she could hear someone talking in the front room. She listened; it was Donald. For just a moment she thought he was talking to himself, but then she realized that of course he was on the telephone, bragging to Aaron.

The Decline of the West

The waiter hovered while the two men studied glossy menus.

"I'll start with a martini," the thin man said. "Sapphire, with a twist."

"Oh, should I?" said his companion. "My gut's been giving me fits lately."

The thin man, whose name was Andrew and who was visiting San Francisco for the first time in several years, sighed and looked out the window. The city revolved slowly beneath him. A pale haze—perhaps it was fog—obscured the Bay and the bridges whose names he had never been able to keep straight. He could not see Alcatraz; he could not see the Coit Tower. Presently the TransAmerica building was passing by, but as a tourist landmark it seemed to him raw and unworthy—like a freshman trying to bluff his way into the fraternity.

"Why don't you bring me a martini as well," he heard his friend Trevor saying. "Or no, strike that; make it a Gibson."

Trevor clapped his hands and settled back in his chair. "Never mind the ulcer," he said. "This is an occasion. How long has it been?"

"The last time I visited the city was eight or nine years ago, with Jolene."

Trevor smiled at him. "No, dear boy, I meant how long since you've visited *me*. Nine years ago you neglected looking me up, if I recall."

"God," Andrew said, "it's been—what? Twenty years?" *Tenth reunion*, he thought. *That was my last encounter with Trevor, and we scarcely spoke.* "Twenty-two years?"

"Twenty-two precisely. Number ten reunion." Trevor lighted a cigarette and blew smoke in Andrew's direction. "How the years whisk by."

"You're looking fine, Trev."

"Surfaces, dear boy."

The two men surveyed each other. Andrew imagined Trevor was being truthful; something about him—a plumpness that was not honest weight, a pinkness to his flesh that was hardly worthy to be called ruddiness—suggested an inner self less substantial than met the eye.

It was one thing to say the man looked "fine"—he did, he carried himself comfortably, he dressed in the fashion. But Andrew could never have said Trevor hadn't changed, over all the years since that class reunion and, earlier, since their college days behind the ivy of a New England alma mater.

"Have you actually got an ulcer?" Andrew said.

"It's how one pays one's dues in the industry—or so I was advised in the beginning." He flourished the cigarette. "But actually? I'm not sure; no one's sure, if the truth were known. My doctor's had me drink the most ghastly stuff—radioactive—so he can snap my duodenum and colon. Lovely couple, glowing for the camera."

"In other words . . ."

"In other words: Who knows? I don't let it slow me down, Andy. One can't let oneself be slowed down."

Andrew nodded as the martinis arrived.

"We'll order shortly," Trevor told the waiter. He raised his glass. "Old times," he said.

"Old times," Andrew echoed. He sipped. The glass was cold against his fingertips, cold on his lips. The rim was fragrant with citrus. "This appears to be a double," he said.

"Double the pleasure." Trevor set down his glass and pondered it. "Do you know," he said, "when I was a child I used to think cocktail onions were made from full-sized onions—that somewhere there existed a factory where Mexican immigrant laborers spent their lives peeling Bermudas, layer by layer, down to marble size."

Andrew smiled.

"What a weeping was in that factory, in my small imagination." He picked up the glass and took a long swallow. "Only way to deal with a suspected ulcer," he said. "Periodic bludgeonings."

Andrew turned his own glass slowly between a thumb and forefinger. "But you enjoy the work?" he said.

"Enjoy? I love it. Couldn't imagine doing anything different. The excitement. Glamour. Rubbing shoulders with the celebrity crowd. If rubbing shoulders is your kink."

"I read about you every now and then. There was a thing in *People* magazine—"

"'Steering the Movie Machine.' Oh, yes, that was nice. And the fey little picture on the cover?"

"I don't remember the cover."

"Ah, but there I was, a tiny little creature in the lower left corner—ascot, cigarette holder. A genuine cover boy. Though I don't recall ever using a cigarette holder." He drained the martini glass. "You know who wrote that piece, of course."

"I didn't notice."

"Fred Merriman. Remember Fred? He was a couple of years be-hind us; we used to poke fun at him—big, awkward boy with enor-mous ears, very slow-spoken. You once said to me: 'Poor Fred. He's so dull he probably thinks an aesthete is someone who doesn't be-lieve in God.' You don't remember?"

"No," Andrew said. "I'm afraid I don't." Though in fact he did—remembered with embarrassment his wisecracks not only about Fred Merriman, but about other fraternity brothers whose tastes he had judged inferior to his own and Trevor's. Merry Andrew, Trevor called him then, always applauding his wit, his affectations. Trevor of Acadia, born and raised in Maine. "I do remember Fred was the one who had all that money stolen from his locker during swim class. What a mess that was."

Trevor reddened. His face changed and his eyes went blank: it was as if someone had struck him and all his muscles had gone slack. Andrew realized instantly what he had done, but it was too late to call back the words. Damn it, damn it, damn it. All those years—he had simply forgotten that Trevor was the thief.

"Sweet Jesus," Trevor hissed. "'The evil men do.' Bravo, Shake-speare."

"Damn it, Trev, I'm sorry. Truly. I'd forgot the details. I'd forgot the whole thing until you mentioned Fred Merriman." Should he grasp Trevor's hand, let the physical contact underscore his contri-tion? Instead he folded his hands together, lacing the fingers. "For-give me," he said.

Trevor leaned back into his chair. He said nothing; slowly the high color faded from his face and his features resumed a shape.

"What about another round?" he said at last. He waved at the waiter. "Plenty of time," he said. "My shuttle to L.A.'s an evening thing."

Andrew finished off his drink. He would have preferred to skip a second martini, and resolved not to touch it. Trevor was quiet again, his gaze somewhere beyond Andrew.

The city went on revolving below them; the mists were thicker, the vistas more restricted.

"You must do most of your work in Los Angeles," Andrew said.

"Yes, that's so." Trevor's eyes focused on him, saw him. "I think sometimes of moving there, staying there. I have a little house in Long Beach. But San Francisco . . ."

"San Francisco seems changed," Andrew said, as if Trevor needed priming on the subject. "Though of course I've never spent much time here."

"Yes," Trevor said, "I suppose it has."

The waiter brought the drinks.

"Perhaps we should order," Andrew said. But Trevor seemed not to hear—only lifted his glass and studied the tiny onion—and after a moment or two the waiter departed.

"A number of people have moved out," Trevor said. "Walnut Creek. Stockton. One begins to hear flattering things about San Diego." He raised his eyes to Andrew's. "Imagine," he said.

"Jolene loved this city," Andrew said. It was true; she loved its clichés: cable cars, Fisherman's Wharf, Golden Gate Park. She made lists beforehand. He remembered her happy fright when a friend drove them down from the summit of Lombard Street. "In a particular way."

"You miss her."

Andrew felt sheepish. "I seem to," he said. He picked up the martini and drank from it before he remembered he had resolved not to.

"You never had children?"

"No. No hostages. And no legacies."

Trevor smiled. "Very fastidious of you," he said. "I've noticed that it's my friends with offspring who seem most queasy about staying here, as if the city had become a corrupter of youth." He sipped. "I'm inclined to disagree," he said. "As an instance: a close acquaintance of mine is involved with the ballet school here. Sometimes he lets me drop in, watch. Quite a talented group—no corruption there, dear boy. Those bright faces, those supple limbs. . . . Though it makes one feel rather over the hill."

"We've reached an age," Andrew said.

"Yes. When nearly everything underscores one's advancing years."

"Something like that."

"I'm sorry about your divorce," Trevor said. "I genuinely am."

"Thank you."

"How close we were once, you and I. Back in the halcyon times of Sunday morning punch at the Beta house, and the girls of Smith and Holyoke, and dreary chapel services three mornings a week."

"We were," Andrew said. "Yes."

He waited, dreading it, to be punished for his earlier inadvertence, for recalling a time so un-halcyon. Instead, Trevor consulted his wristwatch and made a *show*—it was the only exact word—of being startled by the time.

"Dear boy," he said. "I wonder if you'll forgive my finessing lunch after all. Put it down to eccentricity, if you please—and a faulty memory. You do have plans of your own?"

"I'm going up the coast with friends. They live near Occidental."

"Perfect. Then you won't miss me in the least, and I can arrange an earlier shuttle. Here." He put two twenty-dollar bills on the table. "Let me be a proper host."

"If you insist," Andrew said.

Trevor leaned forward, preparing to leave. "I'll tell you what's interesting," he said. "When I met Fred Merriman again after all that water under the bridge, I discovered he'd completely forgotten the locker room episode. It was absolutely expunged from his consciousness. I felt—rehabilitated."

"Trev, truly—I feel rotten." And he did. He felt himself carried back across age and distance to the dormitory, rain drumming at the windows, laughter echoing in the shower room down the hallway, a counterpoint of jazz music filling the stairwell from the floor below. The theft, the whispered suspicions, the confession—here they were in Trevor's earnest face as he stood and laid his hand on Andrew's shoulder. Andrew felt them conveyed through himself, palpably, as if thirty-odd years had never gone by. It was like being waked from a dream of falling.

"Forgiven and forgotten," Trevor said. He squeezed Andrew's shoulder. "Merry Andrew. Now you really have to do something to reclaim the epithet."

Andrew covered Trevor's hand with his own—an impulse—and as quickly took it away; the hand was cool and damp.

"I recommend you revisit the Brundage," Trevor said calmly. "All those jade dogs and dragons and Chinese cats. There's so much beauty in the city, you mustn't avoid it." He dropped his hand to his side. "And don't be such a stranger, dear boy."

Then he was gone. For several minutes Andrew watched him in front of the elevator—patient, manicured hands clasped behind his back—then the slow travel of the restaurant hid him from sight. He continued feeling the pressure of Trevor's hand until he turned in his chair to summon the waiter.

Period Piece

When I came into the lounge she was sitting at the far end of the bar, looking straight ahead, not seeming to notice me. It was day nine of the crossing. The evening before, the ship had left Ponta Delgada, and now we were on our way to Ireland. We would dock in Cobh early in the morning of day eleven. Two days after that, the ship would arrive in Southampton, but I was leaving it at Cobh.

I sat nearby, one barstool between us, and ordered a Scotch. She waited until I'd signed the tab. The clock over the bar read 1433.

"I wondered if you'd recognize me," she said. "It's been a while."

"I didn't at first," I said. "I had a funny feeling I must have seen you somewhere before—some show in New York or Chicago—but it wasn't until your solo number in the second act that I realized."

"And?"

She was fishing—I supposed for a compliment, or possibly a criticism. In our day we'd both gone in heavily for criticism.

"I was surprised you were still dancing," I said. "And then, when you took your bows, I was pleased you were still dancing."

She smiled—not at me, but at the mirror behind the bar and its reflected array of bottles. "I once danced for you. A private performance."

"I remember." My dormitory room, senior year, the last week of spring-semester exams. My roommate had already gone home to Indiana; a lot of people were on the lawn under my windows, drinking and laughing. Someone had a guitar, so there was accompaniment.

In those days you had to sneak the girlfriends in—in through the back entrance and up the service stairs—and it was just as risky getting them out as getting them in. It went on your record if you got caught, and they put you on probation, which meant no class cuts and compulsory chapel for six weeks.

She'd danced barefoot in a pale blue slip, lace swirling at her knees, and improvised steps around whatever rhythms the guitar floated through my windows. She stayed the night; it was the last time we slept together.

"It hadn't occurred to me that when college was finished, we'd be finished too," she said. "Had it occurred to you?"

"I guess I'd never thought about it."

"Just took life as it came," she said. She made a wry face. "I'd somehow thought I could steer it."

She was quiet then, looking down into a glass I noticed was empty. "What are you drinking?" I said. I was reaching for my keycard, but she raised a hand to stop me.

"It's only Perrier," she said. "It isn't wise to drink on the job. Anyway, I don't enjoy it."

I was studying her, I imagine a little too obviously. You know how when you haven't seen a person in a long time—years, decades—you have to fit your last view of them into time's latest disguise.

"What is it?" she said. "Trying to read my mind?"

"Where was it—the last place I saw you? Was that Toronto?"

"You chose the right city," she said. "I'd have been crushed if you hadn't."

"The rehearsal hall at the O'Keefe." It came back to me with unexpected force: a mirror wall, voices and the scuffle of feet, a repetitive piano tune—all of those sounds echoing in the huge room.

"Right again," she said. "The theater was trying to impress an Ontario lumber baron out of some endowment money. We were cobbling together an arty and artful pitch."

"You were terrific the next night."

"What was it?" She was frowning at her memory. "Was it 'Sweet Charity'? Yes, it was. How appropriate."

"I lost track of you after that," I said. "You seemed to disappear."

"Ah, yes." She hugged herself, rocked toward me and rocked away. "Totally a bolt from the blue. One minute I was sane, the next I was a basket case and people in white coats were standing around pulling their beards."

"But you came out of it."

"After almost two years. Drugs. Hours of wise talk. They wanted to do electroshock—speaking of bolts—but my mother wouldn't allow it."

"How did you end up on a cruise ship?"

She fairly bristled. "Agents find the jobs," she said. "And I haven't 'ended up' here, as you put it."

"I didn't mean it to come out that way," I said. "Forgive me."

"I forgive you. I always did forgive you."

*　*　*

WE SAT IN THE MIDST of what a script might have described as "an extended pause," after which we both tried to undo whatever offense she thought me guilty of.

"What are you doing to pass the time?" she offered.

"Not much," I said. "Reading. Having a drink here and there. Watching a TV movie if a decent one appears."

"The crossing must be boring you, if you're reduced to television."

She gave me the teasing smile that had been her trademark in earlier times—an expression that condescended without being unkind.

"They were playing 'Sunset Boulevard' in the wee hours," I said. "I'd forgotten how William Holden first stumbled on the decaying mansion."

"The car chase." I raised an eyebrow. "I confess," she said. "I watched it too—after the show, to unwind."

I sipped my drink, looking at her, still coaxing the girl I remembered from the woman in front of me.

"It's only in the movies that the pursuers never see a car that's just off the road," I said. "They always race right by. It's as if they're wearing blinders."

"They're predators," she said. "They have eyes that look straight ahead and focus on motion. The skip tracers were falcons; Holden was a bunny."

"A dead bunny."

"Yes. A dead bunny."

I looked past her to the outward-slanted windows of the lounge. The pattern of sunlight on the ocean, shimmers of whitecaps on the dark water, reminded me at that moment of scattered leaves on the autumnal New England campus where we had first met.

"I'd forgotten we shared a zoology class," I said.

"And American Lit. You sat directly behind me in both. You kept blowing on the back of my neck."

"I was always trying to excite you."

"And you did. Though you also made me furious. It seemed so public, and so—so proprietary."

"I meant it that way."

She shook her head, as if I were not to be believed.

"You know I did," I insisted.

"Though you were often distracted," she said. "Even when we

were alone—remember? In that far corner of the Union?—your eyes were all over every coed in the room."

"They're probably not called 'coeds' anymore."

She shrugged and looked away. "Who knows how a college changes after twenty years?"

And then she said, "I remember once you got into this long argument with Professor Hall—a boring one, I thought—about *The Great Gatsby*. You said it was a lazy novel. You said Fitzgerald used his characters like a dragonfly skimming a pond, touching the water here and there, sending out a lot of interesting ripples but never dipping below the surface."

"I was pretty full of myself in those days." It was a long time since I'd thought of Hall, who had probably done more to persuade me to writing than anyone else in my life.

"I used to think you wanted to be Gatsby."

"No. I wanted to be Dick Diver." I reached out then and put my hand over hers. Don't ask me why; I knew it was *proprietary*. "And you did your best to be Nicole."

She slipped her hand out from under mine. "Didn't I ever," she said.

*   *   *

"You're still a remarkable dancer," I said. It was the baldest kind of subject change, but she seemed relieved by it.

"I could do endorsements for anti-inflammatories," she said, "but thank you again for the compliment."

"The blues sequence, and that sexy tango piece—you were dazzling."

"Not quite as limber as I once was, but I've kept in condition, worked out every day even—when I was confined."

More silence settled between us. The bartender poured Perrier into her glass, as if on a cue I'd missed. "I'm allowing myself another six months with this ship," she said, "so at least I can say I've seen the Mediterranean. You and I are of an age, so you know the sum of my next birthday."

"They say that's when life begins."

"They used to. Now they say sixty is the new forty."

"Then where will you go?" I could hardly imagine her giving up dancing, always her lifeline.

"Anywhere I can afford an apartment."

"And to fill the time?"

"I'd like to open a dance studio." She sipped her drink and turned a self-deprecating grin toward me. "You know: a school for boys and girls whose mothers want them to learn poise and grace. A little tap, a little fifth position. Those sweaty little bodies—I see them in my dreams of future."

"Besides you," I said now, "I thought the best performer was that singer—the colored girl who did 'Stardust.'"

Her face opened into a genuine smile. "Listen to you," she said. "A 'colored girl.' You're still living in the F. Scott world, and you don't even realize it."

"Then what does she call herself? African-American? Black?"

"I doubt she defines herself that way, any more than you think of yourself as 'Caucasian.'" She shook her head in mock disbelief. "Anyway, her name is Twana—which in Swahili means someone not to be trusted. Just your type."

"I'll add that to my Swahili vocabulary," I said. I was seeing more and more sharp edges of the lover she'd been to me.

"Twana is my counterpart at the other end of the talent spectrum. I'm going out, she's coming in. She's only twenty-four. She's understudied a couple of famous names, but none of them has had the decency to come down with laryngitis. She signed onto the cruise as a stop-gap."

"She's not staying for the Mediterranean?"

"She's flying home from London. Her agent has lined up a bunch of auditions. Maybe this will be her breakthrough year." She tilted her head and pondered me. "Did you ask because you're interested?"

"Idle curiosity," I said.

Her laugh was sarcastic. "Still distracted," she said.

I signaled the barman for another Scotch.

*   *   *

"WHAT ABOUT YOU?" she said. "What's in your future?"

"I'm getting off in Cobh," I said. "Going to do some house hunting."

"You want to live there?"

"I'm going to give it a try. They say Ireland is fond of writers."

"And you crave affection," she said.

"Which I'll trade for the tax breaks."

"I've actually seen your name on a movie or two," she said. "Has it made you rich?"

"Not noticeably." She might have seen my name, but alas, it had never stood alone on the screen. "'Collaborative medium' means the rewards are diluted," I told her.

"Has it been a good crossing for you? Besides the privilege of seeing me dance, and watching old movies, have you had fun?"

"I suppose I have. I was sorry the weather kept us out of Bermuda, but the Azores were a bonus."

"I didn't go ashore," she said. "The island and the mountains looked gorgeously green."

"They were. If Ireland doesn't pan out, I might look for something on São Miguel."

She smiled at that. "How's your Portuguese?" she said.

"Nonexistent."

"Then you should thrive."

She looked at a small gold watch on her left wrist and turned the barstool so that for a moment, and for the first time, she was facing me directly.

"I really have to get ready for my close-up," she said. "Rehearsal's at three and nobody dares be late."

"Maybe I'll come back to see the show again."

"You could do that," she said. "It's free." She touched my shoulder and brushed her lips against my cheek as she passed. "I'll give your idle curiosity to Twana."

I watched her as she went, still lovely in her bones, her movements as graceful as I remembered.

*   *   *

THE AFTERNOON BEFORE, coming back to the ship with other passengers from a bus excursion around São Miguel, I'd taken a last couple of touristy photos. On the concrete walls of the bunkers that lined the quay were years of colorful graffiti that seemed hardly to belong with the other photos I had taken that day: bold, painted banners and coats-of-arms; testimonies of allegiance to flags Dutch and Swedish, Chilean and British; what I took to be exotic ship names, like *Tom Elba, Moutinho, ENS Toushka, Blanco Encalada.* Some were recent, some were old enough to be fading into dim shadow.

Scrolling through the images in my small camera, these quayside pictures were garish beside the rich green of the island's steep valleys, or the paler blue and green of twin lakes where an ancient volcano had fallen in on itself. Thinking I'd need space for real estate pictures when I arrived at Cobh, I downloaded everything onto my laptop, changing into my evening shirt and tie while the imports progressed.

Just before dinner, I took the elevator down to deck five and strolled past the shops that lined both sides of the promenade. Just beyond the duty-free was a florist cart, contrived to mimic a street vendor's display, and I stopped at it—a whim; not anything I'd planned.

A dark-skinned young woman sat behind the cart, tying white ribbon around a cluster of miniature pink and red roses. She spoke in what I took to be a Jamaican accent.

"I can assist you, sir?"

"If I buy flowers, can you deliver them on board?"

"My pleasure, sir."

I looked over the inventory of the cart. Several corsages, two or three small arrangements in pottery jars. A sparse offering, nothing like the arms-full bouquets a performer might accept across the footlights.

"Something like that thing you're working on," I said. "May I buy one of those?"

"Yes, surely." She finished tying her ribbon with a deft flourish and held the roses out to me. "Would you like this one?"

"That's fine."

I gave her my keycard, signed for the flowers, tucked card and receipt in my shirt pocket.

"Where shall we deliver?" she asked.

"You know the evening show? In the theater?"

"Yes."

"The flowers go to one of the performers," I said. "Can you deliver it just at the end of the second show?"

"Surely, yes." She found a small white envelope and took up a blue-and-white ship's pen. "For whom shall it be?"

"I believe her name is Twana," I said.

She scribbled the name. "And from?"

"Just sign it *An admirer.*"

She did so, frowning as she slid the card into its envelope.

Going on to the second seating, threading my way to my table at the back of the dining room, I persuaded myself the flowers were a harmless gesture, no different from a sailor's graffiti—only another way of claiming without possessing.

Crooked

Sarah Elliot's first real boyfriend showed her how to steal. This was in junior high school, eighth grade. His name was Roger Everett, his hair was so blond it was almost white, and he licked his lips whenever it was about to happen.

The first time was on a cold day in early spring. They were walking to school together after lunch, talking, shoulders touching. To get to the Emerson School you had to walk through downtown and go past a gas station, a church, two banks, a restaurant, and the five-and-dime. Today Roger said, "Let's stop at the five-and-dime. I want to buy something."

They went in. The five-and-dime was a Woolworth's, though the name didn't matter much, since the store was almost identical to McClellan's, which was on the other side of the street across from the National Bank, and to S. S. Kresge, around the corner on Washington Street. Woolworth's occupied a deep, narrow space, with two aisles that looked as long as bowling alleys. The floor was wood, unpainted, with a grayish-brown patina of wear from all the customer traffic. The candy and notions were up front; the housewares and pets were way in back.

Sarah wasn't sure what Roger intended to buy, but it didn't look as if Roger was sure either. He led her all the way up one aisle, then around the back of the store under the canary cages, and then down the other aisle toward the front. Sometimes he would lick his lips and pause before some item on the counters they passed. He would pick up a lead soldier, hold it for a moment or two while he examined it, then put it back in its place with other soldiers. At the school supplies counter he picked up pencils and erasers and steel compasses, looked them over, put them back.

After all this, Sarah was surprised when the two of them were back out on the street, strolling toward school.

"I thought you wanted to buy something," she said.

"I did," he told her, and as they walked Roger turned out his mackinaw pockets and reached up his sleeve and showed her two mechanical pencils, a lead soldier kneeling with a rifle, and two chocolate-covered malted milk balls. He gave one of the candies to Sarah, and even though it was slightly linty from his pocket, she ate it.

*   *   *

In June, on the Saturday before graduation rehearsal, she and Roger were walking home from a matinee at the Capitol Theater. They were holding hands. Roger was wearing jeans and a lightweight windbreaker. Sarah had on a white cardigan sweater and a blue cotton dress that went with her eyes; the dress buttoned down the front and had a rim of white lace around the neckline. As they were passing McClellan's windows, Roger slowed down as if he was studying the display on the other side of the glass.

"Let's go in," he said.

This time she knew what was going to happen, so she watched him closely as they went up and down the aisles.

There were clerks everywhere, but Roger didn't seem to notice them. So far as Sarah could tell, he didn't take any candy or toys or school stuff, although it seemed as if he picked up everything he saw and turned it around and around in his hands before returning it to the counter. She wondered what he was after, and so she asked him.

"I just wanted to get something for you," he said. "A little graduation present."

They were in front of the costume jewelry counter, and he stopped her there. He picked up a pair of bracelets, looked them over, put them back. He studied one card of earrings, then another, but returned them. He put one hand to his chin and pretended to decide between a ring with a green stone and a ring with a red stone. A clerk, a tall woman with dark hair twisted into a bun, was watching him.

"I don't know," Roger said in a loud voice. He put the rings down and looked straight at the clerk. "It's hard to choose," he said.

The woman didn't say anything. She half turned away, but Sarah could see that she was watching Roger out of the corner of her eye.

"We ought to go," Sarah said.

Roger untangled a necklace from a heap of thin chains and held it up. It was a gold-colored chain with a single blue stone dangling from it. He held it against Sarah's throat.

"This looks nice," he said, and licked his lips. Sarah couldn't see what it would have looked like around her neck, but then she felt it slide down her skin and stop at her bra and become a cold little knot between her breasts. The clerk was behind her, and couldn't have seen.

"But I guess not," Roger said in his loud voice. He took his hands from Sarah's throat and passed them over the tangle of necklaces as if he were putting something back. "We're trying to find a present for Mom," he said to the clerk, and then he took Sarah's hand and led her out of the store.

"That was neat," Sarah said.

"I wanted you to have it," Roger said.

*　*　*

SHE COULDN'T UNBUTTON HER DRESS in front of Roger, so she had to wait until he walked her home before she could retrieve the necklace and admire it. When she came into the kitchen, planning to go straight to her room, her mother was putting dirty clothes into the Easy washing machine.

"Oh, Sarah," her mother said. "Come here. Let me wash that dress and it'll be ready for your graduation."

She pulled Sarah toward her and started undoing the front of the dress. Sarah was silent, though she resented her mother's proprietorship of her. When the dress was open to the waist it slid off her shoulders and fell to the linoleum floor.

"What's this shiny thing?" Sarah's mother said. She lifted the necklace out of Sarah's white brassiere that was mostly padding and let it hang from her fingers. "Where did you get this?"

"Roger gave it to me."

"And where did Roger get it?"

"At the five-and-dime. It's a gift."

Her mother looked at it. "It looks like a sapphire," she said. "Where did Roger Everett get the money to buy a sapphire necklace? The Everetts are poor as church mice."

"I don't know," Sarah said.

Sarah's mother put the necklace in her apron pocket and began stuffing the blue dress into the washer.

"He stole it, didn't he?" she said.

"I don't know," Sarah said again.

"Didn't he?" It was her mother's warning voice.

"Yes," Sarah said.

* * *

WHEN SHE WAS A SOPHOMORE in high school, Sarah went with
a boy named Leblanc. That was all anyone called him: Leblanc. She
never knew if it was his first name or his last name, but it didn't seem
to matter. He was tall and black-haired. He wore leather jackets and
cowboy boots. He didn't go to Scoggin High School, where Sarah
went. He was at the Catholic school, St. Ignatius, and he spoke English with a French-Canadian accent she thought sounded exotic.

Roger Everett was a thing of the past. Sarah's mother let her wear
his necklace when she found it was not sapphire but only blue glass,
and one day during gym class it was stolen and never returned. By
then she'd met Leblanc, so she could appreciate the irony of her loss.
Long after she broke up with Roger—her mother had insisted—she
used to see him once in a while in the halls by the lockers. Then,
after their sophomore year, she didn't see him anymore. She heard
he'd been caught stealing in Willard's Hardware, and Mr. Willard
had him arrested. The rumor was that Roger had been sent to Bath,
to a special school for difficult children.

Leblanc was entirely different from Roger. Leblanc played basketball and baseball, and he didn't steal from dime stores and hardware
stores. Leblanc stole cars.

This was shortly after the war, when people still drove downtown
in the evenings and parked on Main Street. They sat in their cars
just to watch other people walk by. Boys sat hoping to see girls, and
girls hoped to see boys, and older people who were already attached
or married sat in their cars to see and be seen. If you didn't own a
car, you walked up and down the street looking for friends who did.
If you were Leblanc, you walked up and down until you found a car
you wanted to steal.

On their first date, in mid-September of her junior year, Leblanc
called for Sarah at her home. His hair was slicked back into a duck's

tail, he wore a necktie, and his boots were so carefully shined, they seemed to glow with a dark inner light. He waited in the kitchen while Sarah finished brushing her hair and putting on lipstick.

"He seems like a very nice boy," her mother said softly. "Don't put on too much of that."

Lately the warning tone had almost gone out of her mother's voice. Sarah's father had been home from the army for only a couple of months, and her mother was often distracted. The distraction left Sarah unexpectedly free.

"We're going downtown," she told her mother. "We may go to a movie."

"Be home by ten," her mother said.

Leblanc took her first to Thompson's Pharmacy. They sat in a booth in the back of the store and drank Cokes and traded stories about their teachers. Sarah's were large maiden ladies with thick ankles, who criticized the girls for wearing Tangee. Leblanc's were nuns; they spoke so quietly, he said, you had to strain to hear what they were saying, but the softness of their voices kept the class from whispering and being rowdy.

"What do you want to do?" Leblanc said.

"The movie is all right with me."

"I got a better idea." He stood up and pulled her out of the booth. "Come on," he said. "*Viens*."

They walked down Main Street in the direction of the town square. Whenever they passed an empty car, Leblanc would drift over to the driver's side and look in.

"What are you doing?" Sarah wondered.

"Looking for keys," he said.

They were in front of the Green Shoe Store when he finally found a car with its keys in the ignition. He beckoned to her.

"Get in," he said.

She got in beside him. Leblanc started the car, backed it out of its parking space, and they were off. He drove to Old Orchard Beach and they left the car facing the ocean, the keys still in it. They roamed the arcades, ate fried clams, walked on the wet sand with their shoes off. When it was late, Leblanc stole a different car and drove Sarah home. She would always remember that night as one of the best of her life.

* * *

WHEN SHE WENT AWAY to college on an art scholarship, Sarah heard that Leblanc was killed in Korea, but she was too busy being a coed to dwell on her adolescence. She worked on the campus newspaper, where she created a cartoon character named *Ignominy Mouse*. She designed the covers for the campus literary magazine. In her junior year she pledged a sorority and began running with her sisters, many of whom were rich, and with their well-to-do boyfriends. All the boyfriends owned cars, and nearly all of them had fraternity brothers or real brothers to entertain Sarah. Her social calendar was full to brimming, and on weekends she was almost always away from Northampton, either in New York City or Boston.

Once she flew to Havana with Ginger Pierce and Ginger's boyfriend and Ginger's father, who owned a Cessna. Ginger and her boyfriend were giddy and lovey-dovey and drank too much in the garish nightclubs where the brass sections of the mambo bands were like the war against Jericho, but Ginger's father, Franklin—Franklin Pierce, like the president—was a dream of courtesy and tact and every other gentlemanly quality Sarah could think of. He taught her to gamble, urging her away from the roulette tables, explaining the strategies of blackjack. He staked her at the craps table, standing behind her with his hands lightly at her waist while she bit her lower lip and flung the dice against chance and shrieked when she made her point. She grew dizzy from heat and cigarette smoke; the smiles of the players, their shouts of encouragement, their cries of despair, the feel of the hard corners of the dice in her damp hands—all these excited her. When she felt Ginger's father reach around her to place his extravagant gold chips in some lucky box on the green table, she leaned back so as to confirm the closeness of their bodies and she wondered where the night would end.

This was in nineteen-fifty, and the social and sexual behaviors were complex. It was acceptable for college women to be naked in bed with a boy—Sarah had undressed and lain with boys from Dartmouth and Williams and Yale and, once, UConn—but it was unacceptable for the pair to go *all the way*. That was the great leap; one did not make it lightly.

Sarah trusted that Ginger's father understood the conventions well enough, and so he did. When they left the casino it was two in the morning, the night moonless and perfumed by tropic flowers whose names she could not have known, the air palpable, silken on her cheeks and bare shoulders. They held hands; she called him "Franklin" for the first time.

Franklin knew of a place where there were candles on the tables, a piano and bass combo whose repertoire was rich with Ellington compositions, an ambience quiet enough to talk in. He introduced her to old-fashioneds, made a humorous speech about the importance of the correct bourbon, the precise amount and kind of sugar. He went on to compare the merits of the old-fashioned and the mint julep, weighed the virtues of the manhattan against those of the *perfect* manhattan. He made Sarah laugh at what he referred to as his "bartender's view of life"; she finished her drink, ate the orange slice, offered Franklin the cherry. He laughed and took it from her. When they returned to the hotel, Ginger and Ginger's boyfriend were still out on the town, although it was now nearly four in the morning. In the end, partly because both she and Franklin were already naked together in his bed, they made love.

Afterward, her life changed. It really had been love, and now she spent most of her weekends with Ginger's father. She would have spent every hour with him if business matters hadn't sometimes occupied his attention. When he was free, Franklin took her to Boston and New York, where she had often been, and to Chicago and Los Angeles and Seattle, which were new to her. Sometimes they traveled in his Cessna, but for longer flights Franklin would charter a plane, or they would fly commercially, in a DC-6 or a graceful Constellation. At Christmas they flew to Rome, then back to Miami for New Year's Eve; on New Year's Day they set sail with a friend of Franklin's to St. Barthelmy, and from the friend's house on the beach at Baie St. Jean, Sarah swam topless because that was the way it was done on French St. Bart's. Bared to the light, her small breasts felt cool and weighty and perfect.

At Easter time, Franklin took her to Paris and London and, finally, Dublin, where they stayed at a white hotel in Dun Laoghaire and ate mussels and crab in a tiny restaurant that overlooked the Strand. In every city he bought her gifts, sometimes jewelry but more often dresses, suits, shoes, extravagant hats. At the end of six months with Franklin, Sarah's closets held more clothes than she had owned in her whole life.

After the last final exam of her junior year she took the train to Boston to meet Franklin, who was flying back from a business trip to Istanbul. The idea was that the two of them would spend the summer together—he had promised her Lebanon, "a country so green and lovely and civilized, you will never want to come back to the States," he said—but his flight never arrived. The plane fell into the ocean in a storm off the Azores; no one survived.

* * *

HER LIFE CHANGED AGAIN. During her last year of college she shared an apartment with Ginger Pierce's former boyfriend, who was scornful of her innocence about her dead lover.

"All the time you spent with him," he said, "and you never asked him what business he was in?"

"I asked him once."

"And what did he say?"

"Import-Export," Sarah said.

"So," said Ginger's ex. "Did you know what that meant?"

"No."

"It meant drugs," he said. "Whenever he was away on business, he was flying to places like Beirut and Islamabad. Didn't he ever tell you where he'd been?"

"I didn't meddle," Sarah said. "I was in love with him."

"Opium," the ex said. "Reefer."

Ginger's former boyfriend was named Don-John. He was the drummer in a swing band, and one year he had traveled with the Charlie Spivak orchestra. He wore horn-rimmed glasses with lenses so thick it was like being watched by an owl. He'd been around, claimed to know all the big-name musicians. He spoke of them in familiar terms; he called them Woody and Les and Stan, and referred casually to "the Duke" and "the Count." He also knew most of the girl singers of the day—knew them intimately. You could name a famous girl singer and he would nod and look wise. "Oh, yeah," he would say deprecatingly, "that one'll spread her legs for anybody who's got the price of a drink."

Don-John was often on the road. When he was in town, he lay around and drank rum and smoked reefer. He told stories about the big-band business, the pupils of his eyes big as nickels behind his lenses; all the stories were about fucking the teenaged girls who

168

stood in front of the bandstand and looked googly-eyed at the musicians. The fucking took place between sets, in parking lots outside the dance halls—the girls giggling and moaning in backseats, or pushed, helpless, against trunk lids, or bent over front fenders like the carcasses of shot deer while the musicians of their fantasies humped and cursed.

Sarah didn't much like Don-John, but he let her stay in the apartment rent-free because she'd been Ginger's roommate. He thought Sarah might put in a good word for him with Ginger, who had become wealthy after her father's death.

Every once in a while, when she was depressed, Sarah wished Franklin Pierce had left a will that took their love affair into account, but mostly she simply put up with her everyday sadness. When she heard Eddie Fisher sing "Wish You Were Here," or Jo Stafford singing "You Belong to Me," or—especially—Frankie Laine's recording of "We'll Be Together Again," she wept and thought about Ginger's father when he was alive. She was certain she would never meet another man as considerate and attentive as he had been.

*   *   *

When she graduated from college Sarah went to RISD, to learn practical applications for her talent as an artist. She studied illustration and design and began doing freelance work for department stores in Boston and New York. She did fashion illustrations for Jordan Marsh and Lord & Taylor, elongating the women's figures on her easel, frowning at the suits and coats that hung on hangers beside her while she taught herself to draw textures of fur and fabric.

After a year in Providence she moved to Boston and took a job with the advertising department at Filene's. The art director was a man named Wiley Galvin, an Irishman with a high forehead rising toward baldness. Galvin took her under his wing, taught her layout and introduced her into his circle of friends: men and women in their twenties and thirties who were artists and dancers and writers. "It's an arty-tarty crowd," Galvin warned her, "and some of their talents are puny, but here and there you'll find a gem whose polishing you might decide to take upon yourself."

They were sitting in Galvin's Cambridge apartment when he made this speech, a bottle of Bushmills and a pitcher of ice water between them; it was the first time they had drunk together, and the first time Sarah was able to notice how he lapsed into brogue when he was drinking. He was in his late forties, her father's age and Franklin's, and years later, when she looked back upon it, she thought she might have made too much of both connections. For whatever reason, she stayed that night with Galvin and began visiting his apartment regularly. She soon found that he was not much interested in sex—indeed, he rarely took her to bed unless she forced herself on him—but he was kind and comfortable, more like a teacher than a lover. That was fine; she could cherish Franklin's memory, the passion of it, the material and palpable quality of it, so much the more easily.

Over the months that followed, Galvin encouraged her to branch out, not to confine herself to what he called her "chores" at Filene's. He put her in touch with the men who managed the Boston theaters and concert halls, introduced her to administrators at Harvard and the New England Conservatory, took her around to gallery owners up and down Tremont Street. She did posters and broadsheets for plays and concerts, illustrations for the covers of programs, title boards for productions of Brecht and Ionesco and Beckett. *SE* in the corners of public artwork became a kind of hallmark of visual quality. Pencil, pastels, gouache, silk-screen, collage—with Galvin urging her, she indeed "branched out." She was like a tree devised and nourished by a mad-genius gardener, too tall to be ignored, too full for its shade to be escaped.

She met everyone. One afternoon after a symphony rehearsal she drank cappuccino with Koussevitsky and William Kapell. It was a day she never forgot; when Kapell was killed within the year, in a plane crash into a California mountain, she lay sobbing in Galvin's arms, saying over and over, "Franklin is dead, Franklin is dead." If grief had confused her, what was the difference? It seemed to Sarah that talent and beauty and love and all hopes for the future were doomed on this earth.

*   *   *

BY THE END OF THE NINETEEN-SIXTIES, Sarah was the assistant art director at Filene's, working only half-time, spending the rest of her week in a rented studio overlooking the Charles, not far from the museum. Wiley Galvin was still in her life and still encouraging her "to widen her circle of friends, expand her influence, enlarge her horizons." These were his words, delivered soberly and without accent. He introduced her to a man he thought she should marry—though she was not yet aware of the destiny that would keep her from becoming a wife. The man's name was Perry Adams. He was an older poet—fiftyish, like Galvin—teaching at B.U., his talk full of names like Lowell and Plath, Starbuck and Sexton, claiming a distant connection to Henry Adams. He was outspoken, political, ambitious for celebrity, and at first Sarah disliked him. She protested to Galvin.

"Why are you throwing me at him?" she said. "He makes me uncomfortable."

"You'll get used to him," Galvin told her. "He's really quite a good poet, and anyway, I think you need an adventure—as do we all."

He continued, against her wishes, to invite Adams to his increasingly frequent parties; he arranged for himself and Sarah to be invited to other gatherings where Adams appeared. He was bent on managing Sarah's "adventure" for her.

Sarah tried to shrug it off. She wasn't at all sure why she needed an adventure, but on those nights when she lay beside Galvin, untouched and pondering her relationships with men, it occurred to her that each of the men in her life had been a loner emotionally and spiritually—that she had touched each of them only materially. She wondered if perhaps Galvin saw herself and Adams as soul-mates, if he had an insight into the pair of them that she lacked. How novel to be loved deeply and genuinely! Having weighed these thoughts, she would turn and reach out to Galvin—her hand provocative, her breath hot against him—knowing the considerable odds that he would recoil from her. Finally, on a night when the fog that had settled over Boston seemed also to have obscured her reason, she stayed away and went to bed with Adams, knowing how much pleasure it would give to Galvin.

*   *   *

PERRY ADAMS WAS A DIFFERENT SORT of law-breaker, not petty like Roger, not a thrill-seeker like Leblanc. The war in Asia obsessed him; when he was not teaching or writing, he was marching or attending read-ins or organizing the burning of draft cards. He seemed to have an endless supply of such cards; one day he confessed to Sarah that he had broken into a Selective Service office in Braintree and stolen a handful of them. Whenever any young man made a speech against the war, the draft card he pulled from his pocket and set afire had been supplied by Adams. Adams kept a scrapbook, which held dozens of muddy newspaper photographs of this plural disobedience. He called himself "the godfather of conscientious objection."

At this time of her life, after the march on Washington but just before the horror of Kent State, Sarah was dividing her time among three addresses, Perry's and Galvin's bachelor apartments and her own Brookline Avenue flat. It was both rootless and exhilarating, this butterfly existence that had chosen her; she felt she belonged everywhere and nowhere. *Flibbertigibbet,* her mother would have called her. When she was at Galvin's she was hostess, serving wine and beer, emptying the battered Nash hubcap that served as the apartment's only ashtray, taking in the discussions among the poets and painters and dancers Galvin favored as friends. Death preoccupied them; failure attracted them.

"We see a truth others turn away from," Perry declared. "Poets wear the courage that turns to madness." "The horror that makes suicide desirable," said a brunette young woman in a violet leotard. "That's what Sylvia saw," she said. "I had classes with Sylvia," Perry told them. "She was a witch without a broom." "Driven," someone said. "Damned," added someone else. *Drivel,* Sarah told herself.

At Perry's place she was the overseer of politics and polemic. She marveled that he could adopt a persona entirely unlike his literary self, coldly setting forth a plan for this demonstration, that protest, parceling out the necessary tasks: who would provide signboard, who would paint the slogans, who would negotiate with the police for arrests without injury.

"Cold passion," she told him one night after they had made love. "That's what you have."

"Is that praise?" he wanted to know.

"It makes your poems too logical," she said, "and your politics too radical."

"Screw you, my dear," Perry said, and turned his face to the wall.

∗   ∗   ∗

ONE EVENING AFTER WORK she went to Wiley Galvin's apartment and rang the bell. At first there was no response, and then she heard movement and voices inside. When the door opened at last, Galvin greeted her in his bathrobe and slippers.

"Hello," he said. "You caught me making supper."

Perry Adams was in the kitchen, sitting at the table with its oil-cloth cover, smoking a cigarette. A glass of red wine was in front of him. He was barefoot.

Sarah sat across from Perry, who raised the wine glass toward her. His face wore an expression that dared her to comment. Over his shoulder she saw the bedroom door open, the bed unmade, men's clothes folded in a wicker chair under the window. The air was thick with unspoken knowledge; she had to force herself to break the silence, realizing that if she didn't, she might not be able to breathe.

"I think I'd like a drink too," she said.

Galvin was at the stove, stirring what smelled like a fish chowder. He laid the spoon beside the saucepan and took a stemmed glass down from the cupboard. "Consider it done," he said. "Everything under control."

Fair enough. Of course she went on seeing him, at work and once in a great while at his apartment with others, but Perry Adams dropped out of her life. A few months after Kent State he was arrested inside a Selective Service office and convicted of criminal trespass. By the time she learned that he had served his time and moved to California, Lowell was dead, Sexton was a suicide, the war that had so obsessed everyone was over and done with unless you had fought it and been poisoned by it.

Galvin always tried to put the best possible face on his involvement with Adams. "It was so casual," he told her. "It hardly counts." But what that meant—by what system of reckoning the two men accounted for themselves—Sarah could not determine.

"It doesn't matter," she told Galvin. "We go on." She was thinking not about infidelity or perversity or any other definition of self-betrayal, but simply about the force of circumstance—how it steered one's life off course, then let it veer back, helter-skelter.

She was into her late forties now, and successful enough with her illustrations to be able to resign from Filene's and devote herself to her private career. She produced a series of Boston clichés—the skyline, the Public Gardens, Faneuil Hall—airbrushed to a hard edge and printed in limited editions. Displayed at a gallery on Tremont, they made her enough money to buy clothes she hadn't felt able to afford since Franklin vanished from her life so many years earlier. She thought perhaps she had turned a corner at last, that she was on the verge of leaving the unsatisfactory path her life had followed since the terrible day her lover's plane plunged into the Atlantic.

* * *

ONE EARLY APRIL, unexpectedly, she took sick. Though it was officially spring in Boston, the March lion had chosen to extend its territory, and as she made her way up Tremont Street toward her gallery, new work under her arm, the wind buffeted her, so that she had to maneuver the portfolio like a sail, making constant corrections in order not to be flung against shop windows. By the time she arrived and stood, breathless, inside the gallery, her lungs ached and her head throbbed with pain.

Megan, the gallery owner's assistant, was immediately concerned, putting an arm around Sarah's shoulders, steering her to a chair in a near corner.

"Wicked weather," she said. "You look a fright."

"I was afraid I'd blow away."

"Fortunate you didn't." Megan bent over her, smoothing Sarah's hair away from her face, rubbing Sarah's hands as if to erase the weather from them. "Now then, what have you brought us?"

Sarah laid the portfolio flat on the floor, unlaced and opened it. She knelt before it and drew out the sheets that recorded her artist's life for the past six months. Winter scenes, cold seascapes from a Provincetown weekend, the roiled skies of a looming blizzard. This was the best part, not counting the pleasure of actual studio time:

setting a price on art, valuing that which had no value, bargaining with an agent who knew the market but might not necessarily know talent.

For nearly an hour she forgot her headache, but by the time she left the gallery, she was so woozy she hailed a cab, and when she was safely inside her apartment, out of the wind and bluster, she went straight to bed. Her throat was raw, and she kept giving way to fits of coughing that left her exhausted and breathless. Along with all the rest of it, she had the mother of all headaches, the worst she'd known since her college migraines, and though she didn't take her temperature—where was that damned thermometer anyway?—she knew she was running a fever. She was sure she had never felt worse in her life. The vomiting stopped after the second day, but on the third day her fever spiked and she began to hallucinate. It was an experience so entirely new, it terrified her; she imagined she might be going crazy, and the visions were omens of madness. When they ceased, the world seemed simply gray.

For two weeks she left the bedroom only to relieve herself and to refill a water glass so she could take pills—Tylenol, mostly, or, when the headaches turned unbearable, an expired hydrocodone prescription borrowed years earlier from Perry Adams's endless drug stash. Nothing helped, but her misery finally seemed to reach a plateau. By the end of April she felt well enough to visit a doctor, who chided her for mixing Tylenol and hydrocodone—"Not good for the liver," he told her—but declared her on her way to recovery. "An overdose of New England winter," he said. "There's a lot of it going around." She went back to bed anyway, but at least she felt well enough to eat.

* * *

THAT SUMMER SHE WENT to an artists' colony in the Adirondacks, where she was given the use of a small, square studio perched on a hillside in the woods. It had adequate workspace, a lithography stone and a skylight that pleased her best when rainstorms splintered the incoming light. The space was furnished with a narrow bed, a hot plate, and enough storage shelves for her tools and few belongings. In one corner stood a woodstove for chilly mornings, a modest quantity of split logs stacked near it.

She stayed a month, treating the stay as a working vacation, building her work routine around the routine of the colony. Breakfast was optional; she usually skipped it, waking at daylight and working until noon, when she walked to the Center to pick up the factory-worker lunchbox labeled with her name. In mid-afternoon she returned the lunchbox and stayed long enough to check the hall table for mail and perhaps glance at the day's *Times*. At dinnertime she often came late, to avoid the writers and composers and other artists who gathered outside the dining-room door like cats around a refrigerator.

She was not a social person; she didn't belong with the New Yorkers and the New York connections around her. The closest she came to knowing anyone was on the day she held the obligatory open studio, when a lesbian poet flirted with her. The poet's name was Marta, and she seemed to make a career of attending artists' colonies. "I did Ragdale last summer, MacDowell this spring, Djerassi in the fall." In between, she went home to live with her parents in Atlanta. She stayed in the studio more than two hours, asking questions—about Sarah, about Sarah's friends, about Sarah's work. She tried to be cutesy when she flirted, like asking Sarah what a tusche crayon was for and then saying, "I thought a tush was your pretty butt." At least she never tried to put her hands on Sarah, who was pleased to embrace that small blessing.

By the end of her stay she had produced a series of landscapes, lithographic silhouettes all done in blacks and grays that made them resemble a horizon ahead of a perpetual ominous sunrise. She hadn't minded giving up color; its absence forced her to stretch her imagining, to teach herself techniques that hadn't occurred to her until now. She framed one of the lithographs and made a gift of it to the Marta person, possibly as an apology for her failure to respond to the woman's advances. The rest she stuffed into the woodstove and burned.

*   *   *

WHEN SARAH CAME HOME to Brookline Avenue in July, the city sweltered. She had no air-conditioning, and so for the first time in ages she decided to visit Wiley Galvin, who did. She still remembered sitting in his kitchen on summer afternoons, a glass of wine in front of her, the room marvelously cool and its windowpanes misted over against the heat outside.

Climbing the stairs to his apartment, she wondered what she would say to him after so long. She supposed she would tell him about her work and the plans she hoped lay ahead of her. Certainly she would talk about her Upstate adventures; Galvin would especially enjoy flirty Marta. He'd know Sarah was only here for the air-conditioning, but he'd pour the glass of wine anyway, make her feel at home for old times' sake.

She pushed the doorbell, hearing the muffled chime inside. When no one came, she rang again. Finally, she knocked on the door; the sound echoed in the hallway. He had to be home. Sarah couldn't imagine him going outside on a ninety-degree day.

"If you're looking for the Lowries, they're away for the month."

The voice came from behind her. Turning, she saw a blond woman, small and fortyish, standing in the doorway across the hall.

The woman noticed her confusion. "They have this summer place in Maine," she explained. "I think they go there every year around this time."

"Where is Wiley?" Sarah said.

It was the woman's turn to look confused, but only for a moment. "You must mean Mister Galvin."

"Yes. Wiley Galvin. He lives here."

"Used to," the woman said. "He died."

"He's dead?"

"Almost a year ago. The ambulance came and took him off to the hospital, and a couple of weeks later we heard—my husband and me—that he'd passed away. The Lowries bought the apartment."

How long since she'd been in touch with Galvin? Four years? Five? And now he'd been dead a year and she hadn't even known. "What did he die of?"

"We heard it was pneumonia."

Poor Wiley, Sarah thought. *No adventure in that.*

The next day she went to a Sears store and bought a window air-conditioner. She named it the Wiley Galvin Memorial and installed it in her bedroom for the sake of a decent sleep on hot nights. Sometimes during the day she brought her sketch pad and propped herself against the bed pillows to work, though she rarely managed to finish a sketch before she dozed off.

She realized she was sick of Boston. Late summer and fall brought her a succession of fresh illnesses, some of them minor—a nagging cough that annoyed her for almost two weeks, a brief bout of whatever flu strain was going around—and one of them major: a pre-Christmas attack of bronchitis that frightened her so badly she went to the BWH emergency room and waited two hours to be given a chest x-ray and a prescription inhaler. By the middle of a miserable rain- and fog-filled January, she was ready to say her goodbye to New England.

* * *

FLORIDA, WHERE SHE HAD MET FRANKLIN so many years before, was temperate and high-skied in February, a far cry from the Boston Sarah wished never to see again. She rented an apartment not many miles from the Space Center: a corner unit, third floor, that gave her a direct view of the Intracoastal. Eastward was the Atlantic Ocean, whose waves she couldn't see, though—if the wind was on-shore—she imagined she could hear them. The place was furnished with wicker: chairs, couch, a glass-topped table. On the walls were seascapes—not the turbulent kind sold in New England, but serene vistas of cerulean and sun interspersed with slender palms. An efficiency kitchen offered an electric range, a refrigerator, a battered coffee maker and a blender missing its cap.

The bedroom had a dresser and two wicker nightstands along-side a queen bed. For her first few days in the apartment, Sarah spent most of her time in that bed, nursing the cold she had brought with her from the north. She read magazines she had bought at Lo-gan, and when she laid them aside to rest her eyes she gazed out the window at great boilings of cumulus cloud unlike anything she had seen in the north. They were clouds you could vanish into, clouds from which you would never re-emerge. She was thinking more and more about Franklin; she imagined it was clouds like these that had swallowed him so long ago and would never give him up. So many years had passed, and how quickly.

Once she had shaken off everything of the cold but a persistent cough, she fell easily into her tropical routine, waking early, brewing tea and drinking it on the balcony that faced the river. Escadrilles of pelicans cast angular shadows across her mornings; gulls and cor-morants cried over the water. After the first month she bought an Audubon book, wanting to name the birds that waded and swam along the shore. Stilt-legged white heron and wood stork, ibis and egret, snake-necked anhinga. She tried to memorize them all. Great blue heron, roseate spoonbill; some days an osprey swayed on a high branch of the nearby mangroves.

This was in the early nineteen-eighties. The hostage crisis was over and a movie star was President. Sarah was in her fifties, had few friends and scarcely any connection with the outside world save for whatever the day's mail might bring. Her steadiest lifeline was the peripatetic Marta, whose insistent attraction to Sarah was one of life's great mysteries. Postcards forwarded from New England arrived on a quarterly schedule from whichever arts retreat accepted endlessly promising poets: now the Virginia Center, now Anam Cara, once even a place called Calcata, in Umbria. The cards were scarcely informative. They served only to advertise Marta's literary desirability; Sarah tossed them as soon as they arrived.

She scarcely thought about working, hadn't even unpacked the tools of her craft and art. An easel leaned in the front-hall closet, boxes and jars and a canvas duffle shoved into the corner behind it. She might wake early and alert, ready to apply fresh energy to her new life, but long before noon she felt herself giving way to familiar lethargy. She blamed Florida for making her lazy: all that sun, sky, the distractions of fauna and flora.

Across the river was a hospital, multi-storied and white-stuccoed, looking for all the world like a cruise ship that never sailed. Sarah could see it from her balcony, and she marveled at how the sunrise made the building glow. It wouldn't have occurred to her that she would ever see the inside of that dazzling place, but one morning she awoke feeling feverish, headachy, an oppression reminiscent of the excesses of long-ago nights at Wiley's—alcohol and nicotine and whatever drug it was that passed from hand to hand in his apartment. She was afraid she was being revisited by last spring's flu bug. Only it was worse than that, and at the end of the day, propped against pillows with a book she was trying to read, she coughed blood.

A taxi took her across a causeway to the white hospital. In the emergency room she tried to describe to a receptionist how the book's pages were splattered with vivid red. "Don't make me sick," the woman said. A very young doctor ordered x-rays, took blood, listened to her lungs. "Is there TB in your family?" he wondered. She told him no. He shook his head. "I've never seen anything quite like this."

"What should I do?"

"I think we'd better keep you here," the doctor said. "Just for a while."

The room they gave her looked eastward. If she propped herself up in bed, she could see across the water the balcony where she sipped her tea and memorized her water birds. The distance between yesterday and today seemed nearly infinite.

Doctors, the young one and two others, older, visited her often in the following days. At first they wore masks, but then they ruled out tuberculosis and she saw their faces again. Sometimes they asked questions, other times drew fresh blood, more than once assigned a nurse to wheel her to x-rays and scans and mysterious probes. When she asked—as she often did—"When may I go home?" they had no answer.

*   *   *

AFTER A MONTH, her first college roommate visited her in the hospital. Ginger Pierce was now Ginger Edelmann, wife of an executive at IBM, living in West Palm. Wealth became her. She was exquisitely maintained, looking far younger than her fifty-plus years.

"Don-John had a stroke," she told Sarah. "It was six or seven years ago, and he's been out in Arizona ever since. They've just moved him into one of those hospice places—you know: like the elephant graveyard they used to teach us about in grade school."

"I never thought of him as an elephant," Sarah said. "More like a weasel." The word "weasel" turned into a wheeze that became a coughing fit, the phlegm gurgling in her lungs and throat until she gagged. The pain felt as if someone with strong hands was tearing her lungs like a lettuce head and strewing the leaves of her breath on the floor around the bed. Ginger held her hand and looked away until the attack subsided.

"Jesus," Sarah whispered. "Don't make me laugh."

"I've often wondered what I ever saw in that man," Ginger said, still preoccupied with Don-John while Sarah struggled to reach the water glass on the bedside table. "I think Daddy liked him, and I suppose that's why I kept on with him."

Sarah sipped water, whose coldness seared her throat when she swallowed. "I didn't know him. Not until after you'd broken up with him."

"He was with us in Havana. Don't you remember?"

"I was too wrapped up in your father," Sarah said. "And you and Don went off by yourselves."

"Poor Daddy," Ginger said. "It's a shame we can't have Cuba any more." She took a cigarette pack out of her purse, then realized what she was doing and put it back. "How are you liking Florida?"

"I liked it better before they put me in here."

"You'll be out soon enough."

"I always thought that if I knew I was about to die, I would travel to as many places as I could—the places Franklin and I went to, the new places we'd promised ourselves." She paused to gather her breath, thinking of Havana and Beirut and all the other destinations Franklin wouldn't recognize if he came back from the dead. "How wrong I was."

"Are you about to die?"

"Sometimes." Sarah shivered. "Sometimes I think so."

"Exactly what is it you have?" Ginger said. "What do the doctors say?"

"They say a rare kind of pneumonia. Some weird viral."

"Can't they knock it out, like with a miracle drug?"

"They let me have painkillers if I ask. That's all."

"Are you contagious?"

"They say not."

"Are you a prisoner here?"

"Not of the hospital."

"Then you should get out," Ginger said. "Enjoy some fresh air."

Sarah wanted to agree. "If I were stronger," she said, "I'd love to be in the sun."

Ginger stood up and went to the narrow closet where a nurse had hung the clothes Sarah wore to the hospital all those weeks ago. "It's lying in bed that makes you weak," she said. "And it's good old Florida sunshine that'll perk you up." She brought the clothes to Sarah's bed and laid them over the footboard. "I'm kidnapping you for your own good."

"You know I can't do this." When Ginger threw off the covers, Sarah resisted. The cold that swept over her was more than she could bear; she clawed at the lost blanket, the smooth sheet that had cocooned her. "Ginger, please."

"Try," Ginger said. "Just try."

But she couldn't. Ginger's hands around her wrists were like machines pulling her arms from their sockets. The pain knifed from her shoulders to her spine. She screamed and fainted.

When she came awake again, Ginger was gone, the clothes were back in the narrow closet, and the young doctor was standing at the foot of her bed studying a clipboard.

"How's the pain?" he said. "Too much for you?"

The answer was a wheeze, perhaps a word, though Sarah herself didn't recognize it. She felt like something made out of old paint rags, her lungs burning from turpentine. The doctor frowned and nodded and wrote something on the clipboard. Twenty minutes later a nurse came in and injected her with something she supposed was morphine.

*   *   *

THIS TIME THE HALLUCINATIONS were so vivid she believed them to be real. Ginger hadn't gone, but was only waiting for the doctor and the nurse to leave the room so she could make Sarah ready for the escape. She retrieved Sarah's clothes from the closet and laid them across the bed. This time Sarah sat up without pain, half standing, half leaning against the side of the bed while Ginger helped her dress. Only it wasn't Ginger; it was relentless Marta, the eternally traveling poet.

"Where shall we go?" Marta asked. "Shall we go to the mall? Would you like to stroll the arcade and gawk in shop windows?"

"Yes, let's do that." She pushed Marta out into the hospital corridor, and the two women hurried toward the main entrance. Everyone they passed—doctors and nurses and visitors carrying bouquets of red flowers—smiled and nodded as they passed. "They all look so happy," Sarah said.

"They see a perfect couple," Marta said. "They see how sexy we are together."

But she didn't feel sexy. She felt—how would Perry have said it? "You tether yourself too tightly to earth," he had once told her; yes, that was how she would describe her present self: *untethered.* Ahead was the hospital entrance, the sun outside a blinding rectangle of light she drifted weightlessly toward.

"You go on ahead," Marta said. "I'm due at Yaddo."

And then Sarah was outside, alone, bursting out of the dark corridor into the vivid day, like being born all over again. A dark limousine emerged from a confused dazzle of parking-lot windshields and glided to a stop in front of her. At the wheel sat a smiling Leblanc. *How many years?* she asked herself. She slid into the back seat, and here was Franklin Pierce himself, looking exactly as she had last seen him at JFK before he hurried away to catch his flight to Rome. She would have to tell Ginger how her father was miraculously the same beautiful man they thought they had lost so many years ago, delivered out of the clouds and the sea that had tried to take him away. "I never dreamed," she started to say, but he put out his hand to cover her mouth. "No more dreams," he said, and away they all went, Leblanc driving certainly the most luxurious car he had ever stolen in his life.

The Climate in Florida

Her first week in Orlando, Marianne Corey read an item in the *Sentinel* about a thirty-year-old woman who accidentally shot herself with her own handgun. The story said the gun was a pearl-handled .25-caliber revolver, and the woman "forgot" she was carrying it. She'd gone to the ladies' room in a restaurant near Fashion Square, and when she lowered her pantyhose in the stall the gun fell onto the floor and discharged. The bullet hit her in the right calf. It was Marianne's introduction to the Florida law that allowed ordinary people to carry concealed weapons, and she used the newspaper clipping to ridicule the law in front of one of her evening classes at Orange Community College.

"Accidental shootings must be the state pastime," she told them. "Every day in the papers there's a new one—little brothers killing little sisters with Daddy's gun, kids getting shot in their schoolyards. At least this story was funny, and the woman didn't die."

She was testing the boundaries. The first day she walked into the classroom, Marianne had been tentative, uneasy about the students in front of her—older, "nontraditional"—sizing her up and rolling their eyes when they heard her accent; about teaching a course called The Business Letter, for heaven's sake; even about being in the South. Now, two weeks into the semester, she felt easier—easy enough to assert herself, to express her opinions even though they might not always fit the course syllabus.

When she finished her gun tirade, nobody said anything. No disagreement. No support. But when the difficulties of the complimentary close had been ironed out and the class was over, a couple of students stopped at her desk. One was a frowzy blond girl with unreal eyebrows and mascara as thick as brownie mix.

"I don't bring my gun to school," she told Marianne, "but I keep it in the glove compartment of my car. I wouldn't not have one, Miz Corey. One day I was driving home from the beach and these two boys in a blue pickup were harassing me—you know: pulling alongside, and dropping back, and then pulling alongside again. Laughing and joking and talking trash. I was getting scared, being alone and all. So finally I reached over and got my gun—it's actually my daddy's .45, a semi-automatic—and the next time these boys came alongside I just showed them it. Held it up in the window so's they could see what it was. They took right off; passed me and drove away just as fast as they knew how." The girl gave Marianne a long, solemn look. "I believe before you criticize the law, you should consider that there are times a woman needs protection," she said.

And right behind this girl was a man she'd already noticed because in every meeting of the class he seemed to be studying her, cataloguing her words and gestures, never taking his eyes off her. A good-looking man, fortyish—she'd noticed that too.

"It seems to me," he said now, "that an attractive person like yourself shouldn't make fun of a law that might be helpful, especially you teaching a night class, and even more especially as the days get shorter."

"That almost sounds threatening," she told him.

He looked sheepish. "Not intended," was all he said.

Evan Giles. She looked him up on her seating chart before she packed her briefcase to leave.

*　*　*

EVAN WOULD SAY, later on, after she'd slept with him and they confessed their first impressions of each other, "They all figured you for some kind of snowbird, taking on a business class for the winter so you didn't have to freeze off your tits up in Michigan or Montana someplace." "But not you?" she had said to that, and he shook his head. "Hell, no," he'd smirked, "I knew what you were: a little Yankee sexpot, ripe for the dipping-in."

Uh-huh, ripe, she would think, remembering she'd had three weeks of finding a lakeside apartment, replacing her Massachusetts driver's and auto licenses, driving in the Orlando traffic where she'd learned to count three when the light went green so she wouldn't get broadsided by cross-traffic running the yellow after it had already turned red. Florida. If it weren't for the climate, she wrote her mother, this would be Hell.

That was before she and Evan got close. He'd made a habit of walking with her to her car—the red Mustang she'd driven from Boston with only one flat tire the whole way—starting with the night she'd criticized the gun laws. One thing happened, and then another. Before she realized how fast he was working, she was drinking with him at a blue-collar lounge near the campus, and one night just before Thanksgiving she stayed the night at his trailer, in a bed whose linens smelled of stale beer and sweat.

That first morning, she was awake before him, knowing exactly what she had done and telling herself she had no regrets in spite of past bad experience. She'd showered while Evan slept on, wedging herself into the stall, keeping her elbows close to her sides while she soaped and shampooed and tried to rinse her hair properly under the weak water pressure. Then she'd made instant coffee and stood at the door of the trailer, drinking the bland liquid and surveying the trailer park. It was a world of clothes poles and Hot Wheels tricycles and sandboxes willy-nilly on concrete aprons between the rows of shabby trailers—"manufactured homes" they were called now. She'd never seen trailers this close up, had never much noticed them except on the television news after high winds. Even in benign sunlight a trailer park looked like a disaster scene.

*   *   *

SHE DIDN'T GIVE UP HER APARTMENT on the lake, but she spent more and more of her time at Evan's, driving out Alafaya Trail to spend weekends. Sometimes, a matter of self-preservation, she did his laundry. Usually the two of them sat around watching football games and drinking. The ethics of the relationship—sleeping with her student!—she pushed to a back closet of her mind. It was all so casual and irresponsible, it made the question of morality trivial.

"So what do you do for a living?" she'd asked that first time. "What's your job?"

"I'm in swimming pools. Maintenance. Cleaning. Sometimes I hire out, pitch solar heating. You know: swim all winter." He fished into his shirt pocket and handed her a business card. Evan-Lee Pool Service.

"You must do all right," she said. "Everybody in Florida seems to own a pool."

"It's a living," he said.

"Why the name? I mean, where's the Lee come from?"

"Ex-wife, Betsy Lee Hargraves. We argued about the name. Matter of fact, we argued about practically everything. I said Evan-Lee sounded serious, like we really meant to do good work. 'Heavenly Pool Service.' You get it?"

"I got it," Marianne said.

"It's O.K. work," he said. "Guy calls up, says come put a leaf trap on my Kreepy Krauly—that's a pool vac—and I say O.K. He pays fifty bucks, I get fifteen of that plus the twenty for the call. I make my own hours, show up when I can."

"That's Florida," she said.

"What is?"

"Showing up when you can. Somebody says they'll stop by on Friday to fix something. Then they show up the following Wednesday. I've learned that much about Florida."

He grinned at her. "Sometimes things come up," he said. "Sometimes you just want to loaf, look at the pictures in *Playboy*, lie around and jerk off."

"That would explain it," she said.

"Sometimes you get the urge to go fishing."

"You made your point."

"Sometimes you even got to do your homework, so your teacher doesn't keep you in, after." He stood up, tucked in his shirttail. "You want another beer?"

She hefted the can in her hand.

"Sure," she said. "Why not?"

She drained the last of her beer, handed Evan the can. He carried it out to the kitchen and tossed it into a wastebasket under the sink. She watched him finish off his own beer, standing at the counter with the evening sun lighting him from the waist up. Flat stomach, firm ass. Tall. Nice ordinary profile. She knew what she was doing with this man in his shabby trailer halfway down the highway to nowhere.

"You want a splash of Beam in your beer?" he said. "A little boilermaker action?"

"No, thanks."

She watched him pop open two cans, take a couple of swallows from one of them and top it up with the bourbon. All the while he was humming a tune she thought she recognized. An old tune she might have learned a dozen years ago when she was playing flute in the high school band.

When he came back into the room and handed her the fresh beer, she had to ask him.

"What's that song you're humming?"

He shrugged. "Just a riff," he said.

"No, but it sounds familiar."

She waited. She knew he could see he'd have to tell her what it was, or she'd keep on asking.

"It's a thing we used to sing in middle school," he said. "'Don't let your dingle-dangle dangle in the dirt. Pick it up and wrap it in your shirt.'"

"Oh," she said.

He sat back on the couch and rolled the side of the beer can across his forehead.

"You asked," he said.

*　*　*

ALL RIGHT, HE WAS COARSE. Was that such a bad thing? She had come to Florida at the end of a crashed relationship with a married man—not that the man had deceived her; nothing so trite. All along she had known about the wife, had sneaked around to motel rooms until he moved out, had lived and traveled with him while the divorce proceedings dragged on. Then, when the decree was final, he changed. One night he was her guilty lover, and the next he was using fists and feet to show her who was master. No wonder the wife let him go.

Only a day or two before setting out for Florida, Marianne had a letter from the man. In it he told her how much he regretted what he had done to her—how he missed her wit, "the happy times over dinner," the nights they danced away. He described the two of them as if they had lived in a sentimental motion picture, and all they had to do now was hold hands and wait for the next reel to be loaded into the projector. Her last evening in Boston, while she was packing the Mustang, he had phoned her. "I don't suppose—" he began. "That's right," Marianne said. "You don't." "It's all right," he said. "I'll find you." Was it a promise or a threat?

And now she was with Evan, who drank too much beer laced with whiskey, fell asleep in front of television, and sang songs with lyrics like "Marianne's a friend of mine, she will do it any time." Evan. A man who worked when he felt like it, stayed in school because he was screwing his teacher, and himself carried a concealed weapon—something she discovered one afternoon in the passionate act of undressing him after they'd been out at a sports bar on University Boulevard, the gun clunking to the floor as she tugged at the belt of his trousers.

∗   ∗   ∗

IN THE EXCITEMENT OF THE MOMENT she noticed only that it was a revolver, the barrel dark blue metal, the handle pale brown and cross-hatched, and she winced when it struck the floor, as if it might have gone off. She said nothing to Evan until the lovemaking was done and he'd opened a beer.

"What about the gun?" she said. "I might have killed us, you or me."

"Not likely," he said. "The safety was on. Anyway, it's not a hair-trigger. You got to squeeze it like you mean it."

"Why do you need a gun?"

"It's not a question of needing it," he said. "Not now anyway." He finished his beer and crushed the aluminum can out of shape. "A long time ago I worked at the Kennel Club, and sometimes I had to carry cash to a bank downtown. That was when I needed a gun."

"You worked for a vet?" she said.

"I worked at the Kennel Club. You don't know what that is? It's the dog track, over in Sanford. The cash was betting money. I'd have forty, fifty, maybe sometimes a hundred thousand dollars needed to be deposited. Keep it in the track's safe overnight, bank it in the morning."

"I see."

"Like they say: I was a very attractive target. Potentially." He grinned at her, a sly, sidelong grin. "So I'd got a special permit to carry a weapon for self-defense. When I quit the job I had to give it up."

He tossed the deformed beer can into a corner of the bedroom.

"Those days, I carried a nine-millimeter that belonged to the track. Now I carry a .38-caliber S-and-W. You know what S-and-W means?"

"Kinky sex?"

He laughed and put his arms around her. He hugged her hard, his cheek against hers and his beard harsh on her skin.

"I love how ignorant you are," he said. "It's the initials for Smith & Wesson, who don't so far as I know stick their nose in people's bedrooms."

"So do you carry large sums of money now? Now that you don't work for the dog track?"

"It was a little while back," he said. "When the state of Florida passed its gun law, it minded me how much I missed carrying one. There's something about it, you know?"

"A sense of power." Marianne said.

"Different from that," Evan said. "More like a sense of security, you know? You tell me go do a thing, I know I can do it—no doubts, no hesitating."

"Security, power—it's the same thing. You're playing word games."

"No," he said, "not the same. 'Power' is tough. 'Security' is cool and confident. I reach back to touch the .38 in my belt, I feel easy, on top of things, nobody's going to shake me up."

"Except me," she said. "I hope."

"Anyway," he said, "when the new law came in I applied for a permit and bought the .38."

"And got your strength back," Marianne said, knowing she was being sarcastic. "Like Samson."

"If that's what you want to think," he said. "Then maybe you'll be what's-her-name. Delilah."

*   *   *

SHE BROODED ABOUT THE REVOLVER—how she thought it might have fired from the shock of hitting the bedroom floor—and the next day she reminded him about the woman who'd accidentally shot herself when she went to the bathroom.

"Just because one person is an idiot," Evan said, "that don't mean the law's no good. This was a stupid woman. And sticking the gun inside her underpants or wherever, I doubt she'd have been able to get to it if she needed it. She'd be better off to carry it in her purse."

"Then you never looked inside a woman's purse."

"You mean how cluttered it is? How much stuff is in there? Sure I have." He reached over to take Marianne's purse off the end of the couch. "I don't mean an ordinary bag like this one," he said. "I mean one designed special."

He showed her, holding the purse so one end faced her.

"If this bag was made to carry a handgun, just for example, one end would be open—like a sleeve, say—and the gun would slip right inside."

"And it would slip right out again."

Evan shook his head. "Velcro," he said. "The sleeve has this Velcro closure. When you need the weapon, you spread the sides apart and reach in." He grinned. "Make you think of anything?"

Never mind his references to sex, she was impressed by Evan's intensity—the way he'd given his energy to describing the special purse. It was what she liked about him in the classroom: an enthusiasm that galvanized the other students, pulled them into discussions about tech-writing matters—passive versus active, comma splices, concrete and abstract detail—that would otherwise be boring, even for her.

"Another thing she was dumb about—that woman who shot herself in the leg—was what she was carrying. A .25-caliber piece is foolish; it's got no stopping power. You shoot somebody with that, you've got no guarantee the guy won't keep on coming. You ought to have at least a .32—or maybe a .357 magnum."

"Not me," Marianne said.

"Folks in general," he said.

*   *   *

FEBRUARY CAME—the second semester at OCC—and Evan was no longer one of her students. After class Marianne walked to her car alone. Most nights she drove home, graded papers, made notes from the new rhetoric book she was using. Sometimes she drove to Evan's, wondering what his mood might be. The pool business was slow in winter; he puttered around the trailer: repairing a broken window screen, taking the propane tank to Home Depot for refilling. Mornings he watched soap operas, drank boilermakers, made a pile of empty beer cans in the corner under the television set. He was happy to see her, made love with her when he was not too drunk, but life was different. She thought that because she was no longer Evan's teacher, she had given up some kind of advantage.

One night when she left the classroom building and approached her car, she could see that someone—a man—was sitting in the passenger seat, silhouetted against the rose-colored floodlighting. She froze, was deciding if she should run back to the building and phone the security people, when the Mustang's dome light came on and Evan stepped out to meet her. She breathed again; at the same time she felt a happy "lift"—as if time had reversed itself and Evan had come back from a distant place where she hadn't been allowed to follow. He opened his arms to her, took her against him and kissed her.

"The best hello I've had since last semester," she said. "What are you doing here?"

"Nothing special," he said. "Just thinking about you."

"But now we've got two cars on campus. I'll still have to drive home alone."

"No, no," he said. "Bruno stopped by for a beer, and I asked him if he'd drop me off."

"All right," she said. "You want me to drive?"

"Better let me," Evan said. "I know where we're going."

She got in on the passenger side. On the backseat was a brown paper bag she didn't recognize.

"How'd you get into the car?" she said.

"I took your spare key. I got here about twenty minutes ago."

"What's in the bag?"

"You'll see."

He drove north on Semoran to Winter Park, then turned east on Aloma. After a mile or so he pulled into a parking lot between a travel agency and a sports store.

"What in the world?" Marianne said.

"You can open the bag now," Evan told her.

She reached into the backseat and brought the bag to the front. Evan was fumbling over her head at the dome light, and as the bag rattled open, the light came on. Out of the bag she slid a concealed thing, heavy for its size. Whatever it was, it was covered in bubble wrap—a pink plastic sheeting wound around and around it, the plastic secured by cellophane tape.

"Open it," Evan said.

She peeled off the tape and pulled open the bubble wrap. The thing slid into her hand: a revolver, pearl-handled, its chrome barrel rainbowed under a thin patina of oil.

"Oh, my," she said.

"What do you think?" he said. "It's a .32. I got a deal on it."

"Why now?" she asked. "Why tonight?"

"D'you like it?"

"I don't know. I didn't expect it." She pushed the pink wrapping onto the floor of the car.

He put his hand under her chin and drew her face to his for a kiss. "I wanted you to have it. Me not being in your class to walk with you."

She held the gun in both her hands. "It weighs a ton," she said. "Will you teach me?"

"You bet." He kissed her again. "We'll go to the range together. It'll be like a date—like the movies, only sexier."

"Shooting is sexy?"

He switched off the dome light. "Wait and see," he said. And then, because the place where they'd parked was isolated and the stores were closed, he made love to her—as if the confined discomfort of the Mustang were the most natural setting in the world for it.

Afterward, when she had put herself together and brushed her hair, she took up the gift revolver and cradled it in both hands.

"You don't honestly believe I could shoot somebody, do you?" she said.

"Sometimes it's enough that they know you're packing."

"Packing?"

"That you're armed," he said.

"Armed and dangerous," she said. "It has a ring to it."

* * *

IT WAS ALMOST MIDNIGHT when she arrived at her apartment after leaving Evan at his trailer. The courtyard grass was damp with dew that shone silver under a nearly full moon. As she climbed the narrow steps to her door she could hear the telephone ringing inside, but by the time she'd turned the key in the two locks and gotten the door open, the ringing had stopped. Probably it was Evan, making sure she was safely home.

She put the bubble-wrapped handgun on the kitchen counter and set her purse beside it. In the living room, the light was flashing on the answering machine.

But it wasn't Evan she heard when she pushed the red button. It was her married man from Boston. "I've found you," he said. Just that. *I've found you*, three little words, and the sound of his voice brought everything back to her: the guilty sex, the gleaming black Jag idling in the dark outside her apartment, the man's unfair power.

The last time he hit her, he'd been on a business trip; he said his flight was late, that it didn't arrive at Logan until after midnight, but Marianne knew better. Even so, she'd been worried for him, and she said as much.

"You're not my keeper," he told her.

He had spoken mildly, but he closed his right hand into a fist and Marianne knew by then what was going to happen. She'd braced herself for the hurt—the flat of the hand, the back of it where his ring might leave a gemstone cut, the corrugation of knuckles. What she hadn't anticipated was where he struck her—not in the face or on the arms she raised to protect herself, but squarely and with enormous force in her stomach. It doubled her over with pain.

My God, he's killed me, was what she'd thought. Her breath was gone; probably her heart stopped—just for that instant of impact—then started beating again. She dropped to her knees, suffocating, her lungs clutching at any air, her vision misted by tears: his shoes, the Florsheims she had bought him for his birthday. His far-off words: "I'm going to bed. You work it out."

How had he found her? Her mother, she imagined. Mothers liked men who had money, who drove expensive cars, who were in charge of their lives.

She went back to the kitchen and stuffed the bubble wrap into the wastebasket under the sink. When she picked up the uncovered .32 it was even heavier than she remembered, and it lay cold in her hand. She held the gun by its handle, put a finger lightly on the trigger and pointed it at the coffee carafe at the end of the counter. What next? she asked herself.

It was as if by making her a gift of this shiny gun, Evan had conjured her old, abusive lover out of the thin air that lay between Orlando and Boston. She had not thought about him since Evan came into her life, had half forgotten standing before the mirror in his bathroom. But there had been nothing to see—no cut, no bruise, no evidence she'd been struck. How smart he was. His poor wife had taught him something.

*   *   *

THE PISTOL RANGE WAS IN THE BASEMENT of a gun shop, down a short flight of wooden stairs. It was brightly lighted and smelled of damp earth and what she supposed was burnt gunpowder. Two men were in the room ahead of her, standing at a narrow wooden barrier whose top formed a kind of counter where she could see the man nearest her had laid his cigarettes and a silver lighter alongside a yellow ammunition box. Both men were firing; when each gun went off, it gave a little hop at the end of the arm holding it.

It was the noise of the firing that surprised her: not the *bang,*

bang of the comics, or the *pow!* of boys' games, but a sort of over-loud *pop* that left almost no echo in the cave of the range.

Evan came down the stairs behind her. "Not what you expected?" he said.

"I didn't know what to expect." She looked at him over her shoulder. "It smells," she said.

He took her elbow and steered her along the barrier. "This is us," he said. "Four and five. You're five."

"All right," she said.

"And that's the target you're aiming at." He pointed down range. The target was about fifty feet away, concentric circles imposed over the frontal silhouette of a man. "Number five," Evan said. "You hit a different target, you're boosting somebody else's score."

He balanced his gym bag on the edge of the counter and arranged weapons and ammunition; he handed Marianne a headset.

"Everybody wears this," he said. "So the noise doesn't bust your eardrums, O.K.?"

"O.K."

"Now you load your weapon." He took the revolver from her and slapped it against his hand. The cylinder flopped open. "Here," he said.

She opened the box of bullets, their tips jewelry-gold. She pushed them clumsily into the cylinder.

"If you were in the military," Evan said, "there'd be a whole ritual to this. The range officer would say, 'Ball ammunition, lock and load' and you'd do what you're doing now, and then he'd say, 'Ready on the right' and 'Ready on the left' and then 'Ready on the firing line.' Finally he'd say, 'Commence firing,' and you'd start shooting at your target."

"How do you know all that?"

"I was in the army. What did you think?"

"When?"

"About twenty years ago. When I was a kid."

"That's why you like guns," Marianne said. "Not because you worked at the dog track."

"Just put on your headset," he told her. "Leave one ear uncovered so we can talk."

She pressed the cylinder into place and held the revolver in front of her with both hands.

"If you need to," Evan said, "you can support your gun-hand wrist with your free hand."

"I squint through one eye," she said. "Isn't that how people aim?"

"You sight down the length of the barrel. You line up this little tab against what you're aiming at."

"Which eye do I use?"

"I don't know. Are you right-eyed or left-eyed?"

"Don't be funny," she said. "Just tell me which one."

He backed away from her. "Here," he said. "Put your hands together and make a triangle out of your thumbs and first fingers." He demonstrated. "Make the triangle real small."

Marianne laid the revolver down and frowned at her hands; she made a triangle about two inches on a side.

"Now pretend you're looking through a keyhole," Evan said. "Look through it at my face."

She framed his face. "Bang, bang," she said.

"You've got your left eye over the keyhole," Evan said. "So you're left-eyed. That's the eye you aim with."

Marianne dropped her hands to her side. "If I'm left-eyed, do I hold the gun in my left hand?"

"Not if you're right-handed."

She pursed her lips. "It lacks symmetry," she said.

"Just do it." He stood behind her and encircled her with his arms.

He held her right wrist—her gun-hand wrist—and lifted it in line with her target. "You start your aim above the target," he told her, "and you bring your weapon down to it, smoothly, very smoothly. You've got your index finger on the trigger. You're bringing the weapon down, down, always smoothly, no herky-jerky, and when your sights are on the target you squeeze the trigger. You don't *pull* the trigger. When somebody talks about 'pulling the trigger,' that's not what they mean. If you really pulled the trigger you'd probably also pull your sights off target and you'd miss. Got it?"

"Squeeze," she said.

"Now your aim might wobble. You might be on the target, then off, then on again. So you're squeezing and you increase the pressure of your finger on the trigger whenever your sights are on target. You don't know exactly when your weapon is going to fire. What you do know is: when it fires, your sights will be on the target."

There was Evan's intensity again, the concentration she had admired from the beginning. Nothing distracted him from a point he wanted to make; it was only reasonable, since he had conjured her married man, that Evan be the one to explain the rules for making him vanish.

While he talked, he guided her hand down and over the target. Now he released her and dropped his hands to her waist. "Got all that?" he said.

"Got it."

"Then slide the safety off and go to it."

"You're supposed to say, 'Commence firing.'"

"No. In this situation the range officer would say, 'Fire at will.'"

He slipped the headset in place on her right ear and bent to kiss her gently on the neck.

"Your hair smells good," he said.

She uncovered the ear. "What?"

"I said your hair smells good."

She replaced the headset. "Watermelon," she said.

*   *   *

THE TARGET WAS SO NEAR—this was a pistol range, Evan had reminded her, not a rifle range—Marianne couldn't imagine not hitting it. But when she brought the sights of the .32 down over the bull's-eye and squeezed the trigger, the revolver leaped in her hand with a force both upward and backward that upset her balance.

Evan caught her with one arm across her shoulders. "Whoa, Nellie," he said. He was laughing.

She slipped the headset off and let it hang around her neck. "I didn't expect that," she said.

"You best use both hands," he told her.

"What did I hit?"

"I don't see anybody down," he said. "I guess you hit nothing."

"I missed the target?"

"By a mile. Try again."

They stayed at the range another half-hour, Evan with the blue-barreled .38 clustering his shots in the chest of his imaginary enemy, Marianne with her silver .32, gripping her right wrist with all her strength as the revolver pulsed and jumped and flew with her, her bullets making a scatter of holes that covered the target unpredictably, sometimes hitting the man's outline, but usually not.

Then she began to get the hang of it. Perhaps her wrist and arm and shoulder were numbed, or she'd found a rhythm that gave the gun a will of its own. When she had reloaded for the last time—Evan impatient to catch the FSU game on the tube—she felt relaxed and focused and smooth. The outline on the target had become real. She could read the monogram on the pocket of the married man's dress shirt with its false French cuffs, she could see him standing beside a car—was it the Jaguar?—at the far end of the Shooters Haven lot.

She fired a round and saw it catch the man in the left shoulder. *My God*, she thought. She heard him beg, clutching the wound, blood pulsing under his hand, and she squeezed the trigger again. A hole appeared in the center of his forehead, and he fell to his knees and stopped begging. She fired once, twice, three times. A triangle of black dots marked where his heart was. Each time she fired, her eyes teared and her mouth made the words: *My God. My God.*

"That's it," Evan shouted to her. "That's it."

My God. She realized she'd been saying the words out loud. Had Evan heard them? She wondered if they were like a prayer, and if they were, what did Evan imagine she was praying for?

Acknowledgments

A number of the stories in this collection have appeared earlier, sometimes in slightly different form:

Aethlon	"The Tennis Lover" (as "Quarters")
The Hopkins Review	"Period Piece"
	"The Dark"
The Iowa Review	"Weights and Measures"
The Literarian	"Wedding Day"
Lost Magazine	"The Phoenix Agent"
New American Writing	"Visits"
Ploughshares	"Fathers"
Redbook	"Pillow Talk" (as "His Cheatin' Heart")
Santa Monica Review	"Crooked"
Sewanee Review	"The Climate in Florida" (as "Packing")
	"Petra"
The Southern California Anthology	"An Age of Beauty and Terror"
The Sun	"The Word"

"The Word" also appeared in *The Mysterious Life of the Heart*. "The Decline of the West" was a selection of the PEN Syndicated Fiction Project and appeared in several North American newspapers.

I owe debts of gratitude to a number of friends and relations whose comments and advice helped shape this collection: to J. Harley McIlrath, a fellow writer and unsparing critic; to Dr. Nader Moinfar and Dr. Abraham Verghese, for corrections to my considerable medical ignorance; most of all to my wife, Susan, and her daughters, Kate and Clare, readers who have shared with me the geography of many of these stories.

Fiction Titles in the Series

Guy Davenport, *Da Vinci's Bicycle*
Stephen Dixon, *14 Stories*
Jack Matthews, *Dubious Persuasions*
Guy Davenport, *Tatlin!*
Joe Ashby Porter, *The Kentucky Stories*
Stephen Dixon, *Time to Go*
Jack Matthews, *Crazy Women*
Jean McGarry, *Airs of Providence*
Jack Matthews, *Ghostly Populations*
Jack Matthews, *Booking in the Heartland*
Jean McGarry, *The Very Rich Hours*
Steve Barthelme, *And He Tells the Little Horse the Whole Story*
Michael Martone, *Safety Patrol*
Jerry Klinkowitz, *Short Season and Other Stories*
James Boylan, *Remind Me to Murder You Later*
Frances Sherwood, *Everything You've Heard Is True*
Stephen Dixon, *All Gone: 18 Short Stories*
Jack Matthews, *Dirty Tricks*
Joe Ashby Porter, *Lithuania*
Robert Nichols, *In the Air*
Ellen Akins, *World Like a Knife*
Greg Johnson, *A Friendly Deceit*
Guy Davenport, *The Jules Verne Steam Balloon*
Guy Davenport, *Eclogues*
Jack Matthews, *Storyhood as We Know It and Other Tales*
Stephen Dixon, *Long Made Short*
Jean McGarry, *Home at Last*

Jerry Klinkowitz, *Basepaths*
Greg Johnson, *I Am Dangerous*
Josephine Jacobsen, *What Goes without Saying: Collected Stories*
Jean McGarry, *Gallagher's Travels*
Richard Burgin, *Fear of Blue Skies*
Avery Chenoweth, *Wingtips*
Judith Grossman, *How Aliens Think*
Glenn Blake, *Drowned Moon*
Robley Wilson, *The Book of Lost Fathers*
Richard Burgin, *The Spirit Returns*
Jean McGarry, *Dream Date*
Tristan Davies, *Cake*
Greg Johnson, *Last Encounter with the Enemy*
John T. Irwin and Jean McGarry, eds., *So the Story Goes: Twenty-five Years of the Johns Hopkins Short Fiction Series*
Richard Burgin, *The Conference on Beautiful Moments*
Max Apple, *The Jew of Home Depot and Other Stories*
Glenn Blake, *Return Fire*
Jean McGarry, *Ocean State*
Richard Burgin, *Shadow Traffic*
Robley Wilson, *Who Will Hear Your Secrets?*